CW00500493

AESTHETICA

CREATIVE WRITING AWARD 2024

Published by Aesthetica Magazine Ltd.

This collection is compiled from the winners and finalists of the
Aesthetica Creative Writing Award in 2023, organised by *Aesthetica Magazine*.

ISBN 978-1-3999-7410-3

Aesthetica Magazine
21 New Street
York
YO1 8RA, UK
info@aestheticamagazine.com
www.aestheticamagazine.com

Cover image:
Anne-Laure Étienne,
Tissue and Bones (2020).
Courtesy of the artist.

Special Thanks to the Aesthetica Creative Writing Award Jury

Alfonzo Sieveking, Aliya Gulamani, Ansa Khan Khattak,
Chris McCabe, Emma Newport, Marl'ene Edwin,
Naush Sabah, Nick Makoha, Oz Hardwick,
Sabhbh Curran, Sofia Akel, Susmita Bhattacharya,
Richard Price, Zoë Brigley.

CONTENTS

POETRY

FICTION

POETRY

What makes a great poem? The satisfaction of when a line falls just right? Is it the striking phrases that remain long after you have read it? Could it be in innovation with language and form? Or might it be a sense of meticulous building across a poem, as Naush Sabah pointed out on our judging panel? Strong poems often convince us – what judge Nick Makoha describes as "the eye of the imagination gazing at something that it deems important." Great poems have a strong vision, as judge Chris McCabe pointed out, and as our final judge Oz Hardwick put it, these are the poems you would fight for. Personally, when I read so many poems, I am just delighted to find work that surprises me.

To read the poems submitted to the Aesthetica Poetry Prize 2023 was for us a pleasure. One the hardest jobs of being an editor or a judge is sifting through submissions to make a shortlist and choose an overall winner. It is difficult because there is so much that is urgent – so many poems that are pressing craft, writing on important subjects, or wielding the power to make us laugh or cry. Our job was to find the very best submissions we could.

All the poems included in this anthology were enjoyed and praised by the judges, but I want to mention a few memorable poems, which made it through the judging rounds to the final list. A favourite was *May I Not Return the Same Way I Came*, a poem that builds a strong sense of place, avoiding stereotypes. Not confining itself to uniformity in form, there is careful attention to detailed description and enjambment. Inspired by Gregory Pardlo's poem *Written by Himself*, the poem repeats the phrase "I was born" but moves in a new direction through a different landscape, only revealing at the end that this is a poem about Nigeria.

Thanks go to the poets for the invention and variety of the poems, which are included here. You will find the sonnet, list poem, couplets, tercets, prose poems, a long line, the very short line, concrete poems and invented forms never seen before. The subject matter too ranges from the giving of coats, a dam disaster, mothers, the River Itchen, or the lowly dung beetle.

Inhabiting the prose poem, *From its Insides, a Gift*, describes a group of siblings in a moment of war, when traumas are ongoing. The grandfather's victory over the snake may be short-lived but it is hard won, and the poem leaves us with the chickens in the coup unharmed – reflecting that this might only be – for now.

This brings us to the overall winning poem, which stood out for us because it takes risks. *The Swimmers : 24th November* is situated by its epigraphs in 2022 in the waters of the English Channel. Written in two long columns, it describes two very different experiences of swimming. The speaker on one side, seemingly a camerawoman, chooses to swim, even while she is troubled by loss and heartbreak and considers what would happen if she were to drown. On the other side, we are told a story of people seeking to cross the channel illegally, not a political football here but real, animated persons with dreams, longings and complexities who ultimately do not seem to be destined to reach safety. As these two columns of text face each other, they seem very distanced. The mental health crisis of the woman speaker is real, but the urgency of the people crossing the channel is also deeply moving. What will happen as the two confront each other? What new understandings can be wrought?

The Swimmers : 24th November is complex, daring formally and thematically, and without easy answers. It seeks to innovate on the page and its content is urgent and relevant to the moment in which we are living. There is ambiguity is this poem, and perhaps the best poems don't have to hammer home a point, but instead ask questions. Maybe they command us to wrestle with complexity ourselves and to continue wondering. Perhaps a great poem is a space for wondering.

Zoë Brigley
Chair, Poetry Prize,
Aesthetica Creative Writing Award

Zoë Brigley has three Poetry Book Society recommended poetry collections from Bloodaxe: *The Secret* (2007), *Conquest* (2012) and *Hand & Skull* (2019). She edits *Poetry Wales* and is a joint poetry editor with Rhian Edwards at Seren Books.

WINNING ENTRY

The Swimmers: 24th November

L'enquête sur la mort de 27 migrants dans la Manche en 2021 accable les secours – Julia Pascual, Le Monde, 14th November 2022

França va ignorar la crida dels migrants ofegats al Canal – Laia Forès, ARA, 17th November 2022

The swimmers push their unicorns
across the waves; with rubbery
fingers some plough the fleshy water;
& some – the craving, the reluctant – deflate out
in the sun. It's a roomy playground
for the grown-up, warm & safe &
so unlike *le large de Calais*. She's come
with a purpose: she'll swim past the buoy.
Is he looking at all? So the distress,
the terror of worn-out love. *Why did*
we come at all? The lady *operatrice*
& hubby on a break holiday. She's even
fancied drowning on this golden coast
of the South, so her ghost would haunt him
along the shore like some whacked
jellyfish. A lukewarm, wide tongue
laps her sex, then infiltrates it.
Her mind now languid, flooded, she can't
refrain – until she's too far, too deep,
the undercurrent sucking too strong.
She sinks her face so she can see
but not breathe & sees dangling, tentacled
translucent angels ... but they're an illusion,
not angels but medusas, & she's nothing
to them either. Fear while swimming feels like
fuel. Of drowning? Of losing her way?
Of him losing sight of her? *Could he*
use my live location? Would he
check it? Nature tricked me into
this love, but nothing – ever – came across.

They push the dinghy forward
with rubbery finger tips against
the wave, & crave for room – in
the end they're grown men doing
what grown men do: they push their terrors
on others, kids & women silent &
reluctant. Is it they already fear
death? By drowning? Or is it the cold?
Like inflatable means deflatable.
Then, like lovers in unrequited love
distress they'll text her over & over
(& send their live location at request)
in the cold of the night, but that night
will actually be hypothermia with a dark sky,
& she'll be more than ghosting them, she'll
let them swim, their exasperated
calls with deadly mockery too.
Their sex was an ocean to lap
the shores of the earth, now languid, madam,
weak as that instant of utter surrender
previous to death, their purposeful chests
flooded like Mittanian citadels,
what their parents must have felt at having
their olive groves drowned – like
people seeing their purpose killed
before they're actually murdered.
To those who worm your way under the seabed:
fancy our dangling bodies as your angels?
They are not, nothing to no one anymore.
As there wasn't a lady nor a god on the CROSS.

Joan García Viltró
Joan García Viltró is a teacher and poet based in Cambrils, on the south Catalan coast. His poems reflect Mediterranean mythologies and his concern with nature struggling under human pressure. He is published in *The London Magazine*, *Full House Literary* and more.

13 ways of looking at ghosts

(after W.S.)

I
Where there is one ghost, there is always more than one ghost
perching on the generous lap of elsewhere.

II
Ghosts ride the bus to the hospice, they whisper
there will be an onwards into the grieving ears of passengers.

III
Ghosts take walks in the electric light of dusk
In summer, they marvel at the daredevil-dives of swifts.

IV
A child and a ghost can be the same
A woman and a man see this, but in different ways.

V
Dog ghosts sprint through fuchsia-hedged
fields, play catch with memories of their humans.

VI
Ghosts don't wear bruises, hearing aids
they have no need for IV infusions, wheelchairs.

VII
Ghosts are good listeners
They will wait for you on the landing for when you are ready.

VIII
On the hill of Lough Hyne
I see a ghost lifting the echo of a curlew's call.

IX
They silenced the trees to build office blocks
The ghosts cried.

X
Ghosts host funerals for the animals crushed crossing roads
In verse, they cantillate.

XI
For dear ones in hospital beds chafing breaths, raise the window
offer emerging ghosts an opening.

XII
It was morning and it was raining. Ghost sat in beech tree with blackbird
watched droplets fall like little liquid mirrors.

XIII
As time turns — we will all be ghosts, our hands
lightly pressed on the shoulders of the living.

Róisín Leggett Bohan

Róisín Leggett Bohan is a writer from Cork. Her work features in *Magma Poetry*, *New Irish Writing*, *Poetry Ireland Review* and elsewhere. Róisín is co-editor of HOWL New Irish Writing. *13 ways of looking at ghosts* was first published by *Southword*, *Issue 43*.

a brief history of birds of prey/ she said

were I eagle red tail hawk or any kind of raptor
from the Latin *rapio* – you guessed it – *to seize or take by force*
as though * threatening loving chiding *

she said it & meant it: a birdlike dinosaur survivor from the theropod
period meaning a meat-eating T. rex or feathered Archaeopteryx
of the Late Jurassic era one-hundred-fifty-million – she said

from a perch/ from a stick-built arboreal nest/ talons outstretched
to keen I'd tear any vertebrate figurine down to dusk
* swift dash cull * inescapable victim/ or instead
she said/ a stone slab/ an articulated tile or some kind of tectonic shift

my earthly plates uplifted a billion years back * as alp or butte ridge
orrange *– more than plain/ she said/ the cumbrance of embrace–were I
Vesuvial/ a coital eruption/ the gray or purple of molten phyllite
& slate interlaced with banded quartz – from the Chilhowee Group

of Catoctin Formation/ columnar up the sides of these oldest
of mountains – in my fissibility my beading easily shivered
with the proper tools: * break iron punch &scriber*
she said/ I'd make a roofing slate perfectly in severed strata as such

of my silken cleavage – were I dominated planarly were I fragile
as rat gnawed concrete were I the story teller in some precise
art with twenty names each for rain & snow & wind explicit in
parlance in my oratorial patois I'd tell a score each of anger/ sadness

& love/ the piercing of a human heart/ from my solace in the intrinsic
patience of land I'd draw the gathered multitude a rendering that simple
English could not possibly challenge * in hell of hot/ quinta of noiseless *
were I the *I* in the power * threatening loving chiding*

she said – I never fought/ I let him take me/ fuck me in a starless suburban
motel – relishing my right to it – to my first person to my own
positionality to my own living life/ this/ this is *my story*/ she said

surviving/ surpassing as an elephant of leviathan memory or even bigger better/
Jefferson's incognitum en famille/ protected or grieving not eating
other animals nor caging nor isolating nor torturing she said/ were I a very

young calf withstanding slaughter or the bones & teeth of that massive unnamed
animal found at Big Bone Lick or as well another in South
Carolina – enslaved Africans pointed out the resemblance to elephants –

were I decoder or philosopher or explicator of affinity/ she said or only
myself inspecious self-defense/ after all placidly bobbing my recollective
waves: just a one-time physical thing between strangers/ no victim

no violator   just a Lake Travis trailer park because I could quickie
& a coup de grace drop-off/ busted screen door   *slap*

Mara Adamitz Scrupe

Mara Adamitz Scrupe is a visual artist, filmmaker and writer. She has authored seven award winning poetry collections. Her work has featured in many international literary journals and she has won or been shortlisted for several visual art and literary prize and fellowships.

A Short History of Coat-Giving

[1] In her seminal anthropological text, *Humanity's Anomia: Struggling with Angels* (Chicago: Labyrinth Press, 2035), Professor Jamieson Twigg catalogues the fourteen known functions of coat-giving:

Coats given as rites of passage.
Coats given as means of disguise.
Coats given for the purpose of collecting bullet casings.
Coats given as emblems of faith.
Coats given as much in jealousy as in love.
Coats given at three minutes past the hour.
Coats given as a means of identification in a crowd, or at distance.
Coats given by strangers.
Coats given for no reason at all.
Coats given because the men in the room are greatly stressed.
Coats given in the reigning theoretical paradigms and all the paradigms yet to be named.
Coats given for expressed reasons, e.g., because you're shivering, because you don't look well.
Coats given then quickly taken back.
Coats wrapped about boys who must listen as a man and a woman scream at each other, smacking their own chests. Their daughter is missing. Their daughter is gone.

Gavin Ritchie
Gavin Ritchie, a bona fide Scot with an MA in Creative Writing. His poetry is about art and justice and features in *Alba*, *Bealtaine*, *The North*. He has placed in the Magma Editors' Competition. He's father to a three-year-old girl whom he hopes will one day save the world.

Black-house Fire

I don't recall the place I saw the grainy film. In it, women toiled in black houses in a croft.

Guide Book: *A black-house fire is never, never unlit.*

I watch one check the driftwood roof by running hands along a tarry beam, and smooth the dun-coloured chaff where her girls sleep toe to toe. In the other room the boys lie asleep in a half-circle, their feet angled like clock-hands to a hearth. Their boots lined up are darkest grey, the colour of the mountains. They rouse themselves in midnight blue before the land takes breath.

Guide Book: *A black-house fire is never, never unlit.*

The girls look out with faces pale as a curtained window. The boys faces are the colour of the smoke. The parents faces are the colour of wheat-stone, and their eyes the colour of a summer that is brief, indelible.

Guide Book: *A black-house fire is never, never unlit.*

The girls bring in peat and water and the men and boys eat. There's no chimney in the house and a woman's day is full of stacking peat and keeping up the smoke. On the chaff bed lies a child's suit set out for a funeral. All the island folk are coming. It's the fourth child of the family and their sadness is cold ash.

Guide Book: *A black-house fire is never, never unlit.*

The tiny suit is wispy white, the palest shade of smoke. The parents smooth it out on a bed the colour of dark wheat. They put on clothes for the funeral that are greyer than the morning, walk across the peat and see ravens at the cliffs. Below, the ocean's rugged grave is cosmic violence. The peat is petrel-dark: nothing grows.

Julie Manning

Julie Manning is a poet and visual artist. She has been shortlisted in the Aesthetica Creative Writing Award, the Peter Porter Poetry Prize and the Blake Poetry Prize amongst others. Her writing features in numerous magazines including *Australian Book Review* and *Meanjin.*

Amplified Heart / Missing

Like outer space, you've found some better place
– Tracey Thorn

Back of the Audi / sweating like a bowl of summer
figs / without a note to explain / hot things lose their heat
fastest / what point in the day / will I evaporate

Dad keeps the stereo playing / cassette tapes / this month
it is Everything but the Girl / Amplified Heart has just been released /
Uncle in the isolation ward / a dance music lover / yet to hear it

Hot air around the hospital / fallen lily petals / crisp in pavement
cracks / absorb every tear / the way potpourri masks the rotten
scent of transmissive infection

Mum forgets her Tesco bag on the front seat / plastic melts
into fibres on the backrest / milk curdles inside Onken yoghurt pots /
my sister's Five Alive blooms into an unrefreshing relief

I sit inside my own memory / learning how to breathe
through a tragedy / suspicious of whether this is the small or bigger
picture / of a memory of that day / my sister counts hearses

The same tessellated pattern for weeks / mum's sunken panda eyes /
dad's inverted lips / jump ropes stretch across the bonnet / silent
drives home / Missing rewinds and plays on repeat /

Tracey's words / orbit my brain / until one day the air cools / long
drives stop / red ribbon on mum's jacket / reminds me / he is
with all his friends now / dancing / on whatever new planet he picks

---

Sophia Rubina Charalambous
Sophia Rubina Charalambous is a Cypriot-Kashmiri journalist and writer, born and raised in London. Her poetry is forthcoming and published in *Bad Lilies*, *Magma*, *streetcake magazine*, *Tentacular* and *Visual Verse*, amongst others. She is working on her first pamphlet.

The Anxiety of House Keys

You wake shivering
the wrong month off your skin.

The shower is grotto-cold,
you brush your teeth with cereal.

You slurp houseplant food,
gnaw on Lego bricks.

Unpaid bills stain the dining table,
you feed other people's pets.

Important emails scream
from the confines of your inbox.

Colleagues treat you
like a fracture that never heals.

Every birthday is a piñata
of disappointment,

people fling looks like hail.
You collect them like baby teeth.

You always get crumpled swans
instead of cards. They never fly.

Once, you dropped the house keys
in the aquarium to see what might hatch.

Christian Ward
Christian Ward is a UK-based poet with recent work in *Red Ogre Review*, *In Parentheses*, *Rainbug Poetry Review* and *Tin Can Poetry*, amongst others. In 2023, he was shortlisted for the Ironbridge Poetry Competition and won the Cathalbui Poetry Competition.

Anyone's Dust

—following the Kakhovka Dam blast

I'm distanced, speechless. My tongue
will not reach the front line of my teeth.

People crouch on sudden rooftop islands
in Kherson where the Dnipro widens.

I've got my hat on in the kitchen. When
did that happen? Am I going

somewhere? There, an emergency
train came in. Some made it on.

I've lowered my lids. I know, had I
grown into the skin of any

one of those saboteurs, I'd have planted
the same bomb. And, suckled

on twisted history, I'd aim the missiles
to pulverize my neighbors' hospitals.

I'd've been guzzling other facts.
But on screen at my table, an old woman,

to her shins in brown water in her house,
huddles two lean dogs trying to climb her

out of the icy wash. Here, June sun
spills through the panes and drenches

bright the ten million specks that float
and sink like silt or ash in the air—stunned

powder of things. Each tumbling
fleck of this dust could be anyone's.

Jed Myers

Jed Myers is author of *Watching the Perseids* (Sacramento Poetry Center Book Award) and the forthcoming *Learning to Hold* (Wandering Aengus Press Editors' Award). His writing is in *Rattle*, *The Poetry Review* and more. He lives in Seattle, where he edits the journal *Bracken*.

Blossoms

Outside someone is thump

thump   thumping

a basketball, round and full,

like, am I supposed to say? a heart

is? — once was?—

can be? Last night, awake, at 3 AM,

I pretended I was back in my apartment

behind the fish taqueria where my husband and I first hooked

up. Back when dreaming

and not weeping was

our second language. We had so many friends,

not dead yet. Though it's true

our daughter—small octopus of surprise—hadn't been born And—

should I believe

more or less in the future now? Now,

an afternoon lull, stuttering

birds. So *this*—

one day last May

I planted wildflower seeds

and the next day,

more, and more
the next,

next and next,

just in case,

and then suddenly—

after staring at the earth for so long—

at what has been buried there...—

is what passes

for joy now?

Fay Dillof

Fay Dillof's poetry is in *Best New Poets, Gettysburg Review* and elsewhere. She has been awarded the Milton Kessler Memorial Prize and the Dogwood Literary Prize. Fay lives with her husband and daughter in Northern California where she works as a psychotherapist.

CODEX DREAM

You're asleep
in a forest
of blue trees
You're lying down
inside a clearing
I'm there, in the circle,
watching you sleep
but
I'm also
somewhere
colder
I'm closing
and opening my eyes
inside a cloud
I'm on top of
a mountain
trying
to tell you
some urgent piece
of news - that *death*
has no terrors
but it does have,
for instance,
a lion
walking slowly
through the forest
of blue trees

Now I'm in a petrol station
where you buy me
a packet
of Polos
It's been years
since my last
Polo!
Your palm
is a bright
spark
beneath the LED
& further out
the horizon
rumbles
Headlights
fill up
the lower
fractus clouds
No essence can exist without
its concrete being,
so, yes -
I'm on the asphalt
But I'm also
walking

backwards into
a cool ring
of stars
Behind
the building
Over
the road
Into
a field of cornflowers
Yes,
I'm watching
from behind
the blue trees
while a lion
without features
comes slowly,
softly,
to eat
a shining
Polo
from your hand

Lucie Richter-Mahr

Lucie grew up in Edinburgh and Berlin and now lives in London. She is interested in the poetics of translation and conservation and has previously held residencies at two literary archives. Her work has appeared in *Propel Magazine*, *Lighthouse Journal* and is forthcoming in *Magma*.

Fingerprint

After Joanne Burns, 'Keyhole'

Wearing the night like the sudden flare of eyes
before the microphone in *Blue Velvet*, delicate
as phosphorus before a match; a fingerprint
on blu-tack. like Tutankhamun's death-mask,
eight little capillaries in the corner of each eye.
a painted fingernail, a capsule, new blue meds;
those '90s colours named after the four horsemen.
the gazebo in The Dead Zone silenced by snow.
like your lipstick ten years after your death, a raised
rash on my lips. *the first night I took my emergency*
meds I watched moths pour from the wall as if from the
entrance of a cave. wearing the night like the truth.
flapping, ever-present. a black plastic sack
tied to four sticks in a migrants' camp that once
was a strip of beach.

Wes Lee

Wes Lee lives in Te Whanganui-a-Tara Wellington, Aotearoa New Zealand. She has three poetry collections and has been published in numerous places. She won the Heroines/Joyce Parkes Women's Writing Prize (2022). Fingerprint was first published by *Westerly, 68.1.*

From its Insides a Gift

Commotion in the coop, hens up in the air, clucking a riot. A viper stole through a snag in the wire. The roosters cackle and shriek, spreading their flightless wings. My father and his four sisters gather by the pen, watch the eggs laid bare. It is wartime, there is famine. They've lived through rebels sieging their home. Seen their uncle hanged by his feet, lashed to his last, soiled breath. Know about shadows hiding in the mountain, slithering out to ravage and devour. They will each go on to make their own hard fortunes, have children, teach us about the warm, brittle abundance of the world. But right now, they wait for their grandfather who hurtles out of the shack with shotgun and a dagger, the same gun he wielded in two wars, for his country, for his family, his plot. The same knife he used to slaughter lambs, on those fat, pre-war days gladdened by the sun, oranges buxom on the boughs, enough to fell and feed the loam. The same man who saw his son tortured to death and never spoke another sentence. Here he is now, shooting the viper, slicing off its head, shaking the writhing beast by the tail. From its insides a gift: eleven slimy, intact eggs the children scoop for a peasant's feast of yolk and oil hissing on the fire. The snake skinned for their seamstress mother,the chickens safe for another hour, venom fangs buried for luck under the cypress.

Vasiliki Albedo

Vasiliki Albedo's poems have appeared in *The Poetry Review*, *Poetry London*, *Oxford Poetry*, *The Rialto*, *Magma* and elsewhere. She has been commended in the National Poetry Prize and won the Poetry Society's 2022 Stanza Award and Poetry International's tiny chapbook prize.

Gift

Gifts for the dying recommended foot cream.
But I bought you a butter dish.
There was comfort in butter,
soft but solid, cradled in utilitarian china.

We tried to add weight to your thin frame,
ate mash and hot cross buns in bed,
left the curtains drawn, licked knives,
brushed crumbs from dirty sheets.

The cost of your new glasses snagged
as we made calculations for life afterwards.
We loved like strangers, hiding
from mutual disappointments.

I regret the longevity of that gift,
its white cow still innocently grazing on top.
I leave it clean and empty by the bread bin.
Sometimes I lift and replace the lid.

Helen Scadding

Helen is a South Devon poet. In 2022, she was selected by Literature South West as an emerging writer. Her work features in *Cerasus*, *Ink Sweat & Tears*, amongst others. Her debut pamphlet, *Sand on the Stairs* is out with Grey Hen. *Gift* was first published by *Raceme*.

Grasse, Provence

We swim mostly, or scuttle in the shadows
of her grandmother's house, its dark *armoires*,
embroidered curtains, lavender by the window
that keeps scorpions out. The day builds

its heat. Geneviève's mother sends us for siesta
but we make perfume from rose petals, stripping
the buds to a stalk, bruising the waxy peelings
under water till they drown in their own scent.

At night we listen in our narrow beds. Something
runs over my feet like a lizard, or a small snake,
but it's a cricket still as the dark with his legs
tightly folded when we pull back the sheets.

Sometimes the sky breaks open, brings our skin
to the surface of its own dream, and every time
it rains like this, a hundred dry black worms
come up, crowd the path, are crushed underfoot.

We go topless because Geneviève says we must
and *it's the south of France and who wears*
clothes here? We are twelve, it is August
and we run, light as the dust under our sandals

kicking up as we pass the farmhouse, and the boys
who live there come out, ask us how old we are.
We stand there, silent, Geneviève well-formed
as Venus on her shell breezing on to the shores

of womanhood, my bare chest narrow, flat,
caught in a perpetual childhood I can't shake off.
Treize, she says, taking aim,
her birthday five months off, three days before

mine, her Sagittarius bold now to my Capricorn.
Et toi? they say. But later we will head back, smoke
Consulates in a pinewood dip behind the house,
inhale menthol, slow and green like a sweet.

Lesley Sharpe

Lesley Sharpe teaches literature and creative writing in London. Her poems, reviews and essays have been published in several journals and anthologies. She cofounded *Lodestone Poets* and is a member of *Red Door Poets*. From 2017-2021, she edited the journal *Heron*.

If my mother had a retrospective at the V&A

Camo, 1978 (wool)

An army green jumper knitted in four
squares for my brother's Action Man
who literally lost his shirt in a
parachute accident off the flat roof.

Wedding Flowers, 1980 (cotton)

A string of crocheted daisies cut from
my mother's wedding dress and sewn
on my communion dress to make it—
and by extension me—less plain.

Cat's Eye, 1981 (polyester)

Carrying bag for marbles made from
old brown curtains. According to my
marble champion brother it was as
strong as a saddle bag.

Gold, 1981 (satin, rope)

A red satin cloak for my Nativity
debut as Melchior, tied around my
neck with a length of rope which until
that point was securing a drape.

Rabbit, 1988 (wool, plastic, thread)

A collaboration with my younger sister
who forgot to finish or even start her
knitting project, complete with odd
button eyes and a wry smile.

Now You See It, 1985 (cotton percale)

One of her finest achievements. A
self-proclaimed invisible mending
of a Woodbine cigarette burn in my
grandmother's quilt from America.

Liz Houchin
Liz Houchin lives in Dublin and holds a Masters in Creative Writing from University College Dublin. In 2021, Her *Anatomy of a Honey girl (poems for tired women)* was published by Southword. She was Poetry Ireland's poet-in-residence at the Scottish Poetry Library.

In praise of dung-beetles

When I first watched one toiling over the sand,
dwarfed by the dried meatball of faeces
rolling in a bee-line despite the obstacle course
of dead leaves and stones in the way,

what immediately came to mind was lugging
the wheelbarrow after mucking out the horse,
and slogging away at night so some bullshitter
of a boss could get his performance bonus.

But then I noticed it head-butting the ground
as the hydraulic hind-legs reversed uphill –
a climber scaling Everest the hard way,
a saint choosing to be crucified upside-down –

and had to replay the narrator's words,
some dung-beetles can haul over a thousand times
their body mass – the equivalent of me dragging
six double-decker buses without breaking sweat.

So let us marvel at these little removal men
going about their business, put the exoskeleton
on every coat-of-arms, and pray that if
one creature survives the hell of climate change,

it is this unsung hero – to clean up the mess
we've made and bury its harvest underground,
so that long after we've scuttled off to extinction,
something – just something – might grow.

Will Kemp
Will Kemp has won numerous competitions, including the Keats-Shelley Prize and Envoi International. He has four collections published and has had poems in *Magma*, *The North*, *The Guardian* and *The Rialto*. He teaches Creative Writing at the University of York.

Inbox

Spend Xmas On The Royal Yacht Britannia
Prick-Hungry Debutants Are Waiting For Ya
Apartments Selling Now In Sunny Luton
Melt Fat From All Your Suffocating Organs

Secret Guaranteed To Make Her Squirt
Pressure Hose Blasts Off All Kinds Of Dirt
Astounding Penis Growth In Just Ten Days
Mobile Zoom For Photos That Amaze

Successful People Follow This Life Hack
Personality Test Can Prove You're Not To Blame
All Your Problems Solved Or Money Back
Maximise Your Income, Sex and Fame

Porn Star Reveals Steamy G-spot Secrets
Apple Cider Vinegar Removes Regrets

Suzanna Fitzpatrick
Suzanna Fitzpatrick's work has been widely published and aired on BBC Radio 4. In 2019 she was shortlisted for the Bridport Prize. In 2023 she was third in the Shepton Snowdrops Competition. Her second forthcoming pamphlet, *Crippled* is with Red Squirrel Press.

Lilias

My mother was a beauty: a snowstorm in summer,
the whoosh of Marilyn Monroe's skirts, a lily
squandering her brightness, skin like Grace Kelly,
but a waning moon, T.B., ghost in the mirror,
a blank page others scribbled on, a doubt,
a melting glacier, a porcelain hairline crack
filled with Kintsugi gold, Diazepam, Prozac,
white sugar, white noise, a white-out.
Rigid in death, her mouth was a black hole
I shrank from, her hands claws, her hair
greasy but she was a carapace, harmless, empty.
Whatever it is that is life, her spirit or soul
was now air, immanent, in the atmosphere,
in the silence before dawn, the light on the sea.

Stephanie Green

Stephanie Green's most recent pamphlet, *Ortelius' Sea-Monsters*, is the winner of the Alastair Reid Prize, 2023. Her poetry / sound walks have appeared in Berlin and the latest, *Rewilding* at the Orkney Nature Festival. In 2023, she won second prize in the Poetry Wales Award.

Instructions for writing to your sister

Instead of *I*, write *weather.*
Instead of *you*, write *weather.*
Instead of *how are you?*, write *how's the weather?*
Instead of *tired*, type *fine.*

Do not think about the last time
that you saw her.

(She was very thin)

Instead of *years*, write *soon.*
Instead of *when*, write *soon.*
Instead of *why*, write *yes.*

Avoid breathing (too fast)

Instead, pause
and read a stranger's argument
on Twitter.

Instead of *he is ill*
Write *all good here*

Instead of *he has died*
Write *all good here*

Instead of *they have gone*
Write *all good here!*

If you are distracted, you may pause again
and walk around the kitchen.

Do not write *I don't*
understand
Do not write *leave*

Do not write: *is he*
reading this?

instead: add an exclamation mark
to your last sentence;

if you must, consider
an ellipsis...

Instead of *hope* write *yes*
Instead of *love* write *love*

Maya Caspari

Maya Caspari's work features in magazines including *Butcher's Dog* and *The Poetry Review*. She has been longlisted in the National Poetry Competition and highly commended in the Forward Prizes. *Instructions for writing to your sister* was first published in *Ambit*.

Interview with Dolores Schiller

"No," she said smiling, "no."
-Lolita

What are you hiding?
Prey that scatters strips of itself
Why do you grin so?
to throw the scenting hounds off track.
So you're married now.
On a date with expiration I wore mother's wedding dress.
Expecting, too.
Rose veal. Girlmeat. When the butcher steps to the auction block, all the animals flock to his window to watch.
Who's watching?
This is the window.
Are you praying for a son?
I hope you don't have daughters.
You used to be so sweet.
Youth's acid. The curdled mind.
Such a peach.
Bored to the pit.
What broke your heart?
Such cyanide.
Your life?

On the back of the carton whose blackedout face.
Speaking of life, how is your sex life?

Sorry wrong question. State your name for the record?
My name is
Your other one.

Go on. Did you think if you denied it wouldn't be yours.

Say it then. Call me the name you think I am.

I knew you couldn't.

Or take a guess, since you know me so well, and I'll tell you if you get close. And if I get it right?

You won't.

Carmen on the silent phonograph.

Motel rug eating bruised kneeknobs.

Knock knock with a monkey's paw.

Needle on mileage ticks up and up like a pinky taps pried thighs.

Who's there?

Witch trial, first thirty days free. Live fish fillet. Fig eats wasp on live tv! Figment of a wet dream. Dreamscape bugs its privacy. Tallies chalk each walled-in sleep. Every room a new gravestone. Corrosion. Shotgun. Acid trip. The cry of a calf called to slaughter.

No, no. Sweeter than that. Like the bell around its neck.

Yesol Kim

Yesol Kim is a student of literature. Her poems have been published in *Southword* as well as *Red Wheelbarrow*. She lives in New York.

Inventory: Things You'll Find When She Dies

(3) x tubes of Carmex cherry lip balm: (1) in the right pocket of her raincoat, nestled among a once-activated personal attack alarm and a shopping list that reads: WINE, GOUDA, CAT FOOD, EYELINER, (1) that disappeared through the hole in the lining of her Prada handbag, (1) in the purple fruit bowl that has never held fruit but instead served as a convenient cauldron into which she would throw all miscellaneous objects that did not have an assigned place. A handwritten victim impact statement (6 x A4 pages, double-sided). The wardrobe door propped open with *The Morning Star* by Karl Ove Knausgaard (hardback, unread). A pile of green dust that was once a lemon. A leaflet about *Understanding Your Depression*. Blood and/or mahogany hair dye on the walls. A letter from the Met that states, "No further action to be taken against [redacted]. All charges dropped due to lack of evidence." A line of white snow on a copy of *Vogue*. (9) x empty vodka bottles. An article printed off the internet titled: *What To Do When Your Rapist Gets Away With It*. A paring knife wrapped in a bloody tea towel. A vial of Bio-Oil 'to reduce the appearance of scarring.' A rosary blessed by Pope John Paul II. The leather armchair that held her while she electively miscarried. Blood and/or mahogany hair dye on the carpets. Her Hit-List, consisting of only one name. A hot pink fake tanning mitt (unused/unwashed since summer 2019). A rare Black Ibex horn, weighty enough to crack a man's skull. A tangle of leggings. Custard Cream crumbs in the bedding. A suitcase full of fancy dresses that she can't squeeze herself into anymore. (11) x laxatives. A Phillips screwdriver under her pillow. Keys to a house she hasn't lived in for two decades. Blood and/or mahogany hair dye on the ceilings. A damp box of matches. A half-eaten burrito (extra cheese, extra guac, extra jalapeños). (16) x max strength appetite suppressants. A freezer that desperately needs defrosting. A sticky I Ching card lying face down underneath the coffee table (Oracle #22). A 'Sorry You're Leaving' card from her employer that says *YOU ARE TOTES AMAZE!!!* on the front in an aggressively glittery neon font. (1) x envelope containing the cremated remains of her darling cat. A near-full sharps box (N.B. used needles to be disposed of according to local authority guidelines). The "lucky" heels she wore when she'd strip over webcam to pay her bills/fund her habit (EU size 36, perfect condition, only ever worn indoors). An attachment nozzle that fits a hoover she has never owned. A length of hosepipe, though she's never had a garden. A letter from her local mental health team confirming that she is "on the waiting list for PTSD therapy and can expect to receive an appointment date within 18-24 months." Blood and/or mahogany hair dye on the doors. (4) x thirsty cacti. (256) x cigarette butts. A dead spider plant. A dusty yoga mat. A post-it note dated 02/07/2020 that reads: I CAN'T FUCKING DO THIS ANYMORE :(~~Enough psychotropic medications to obliterate herself (stockpiled~~

~~and stored in the XXL Ikea bag)~~. (106) variations of *I'm sorry for your loss.* (79) x *This is so sad.* (63) x *omg.* (41) x *She was so young.* (28) x *I had no idea she was struggling.* Please feel free to take whatever you want from the above list. She didn't/doesn't need any of it.

HLR

HLR is the author of *History of Present Complaint* and *EX-CETERA*. In 2021, she was commended in the *National Poetry Competition* and won the *Desmond O'Grady Poetry Competition*. Her work is in *The London Magazine*, *Poetry Wales*, and others.

Left the Hotel that Fema Stopped Paying for on Friday

ended up at a shelter   after-action making the president
look bad   hibiscus yawns
on a once-road
baked in clay   cabo rojo to brooklyn
trickle of feet

is dew drip   this is the first morning
of homelessness   making the president look
bad   my families everywhere   you see
thaliana and her son facetiming tio cruz on the curb
sol   our grand marshall

cries in spanish in the wake   making the president look bad   in a warning
by the unsung   agency in the parade
in a hotel lobby   by the airport
there is nowhere to warm   churn a family-laugh
there ain't goodwill   for evicted psalms   pinned

making the president   look
bad   blue birds saying everything   they heard from
someone else   the rent late
displaced on the balls of feet   trauma for thunder
bruno lying on asphalt   emergency lane

and we worry for the length of   rest in a blanket of sirens
and the atlantic ocean   ruins
and they build their beacon   and cause the brick
tower to deteriorate   and they lit a donation and welcomed
the street light   and ain't it hard just to live?

Karl Michael Iglesias
Originally from Milwaukee and a graduate of the University of Wisconsin, Karl's work is in *Brooklyn Review, The Florida Review* and more. In 2022, he was shortlisted for the *Robert Phillips Chapbook Prize*. His chapbook, *CATCH A GLOW*, is with Finishing Line Press.

May I Not Return the Same Way I Came

After Gregory Pardlo

I was born head first on a Thursday night into the burn
of a kerosene lantern, its shy flame sighing my name.
I was born blinking at the glint of fireflies, fast rats lazing
inside stew pots, croaking choir of drunk uncles at wake ceremonies,
the occasional sunshower. I was born a number
among fervent eyes: children thick-coated in Vaseline – polish
for feeble limbs poverty feasts on, poverty familiar as the savor
of fresh butter bread at breakfast. I was born to red clay roads,
King James Versions, yellow mangoes, swarms of cheerful mosquitoes,
salt on doorsteps and room corners, moonlight playdates, onion juice squeezed
into the eyes of a convulsing infant, all your neighbors' secrets,
no pet cats – they house witches' spirits, naked husband and wife
fighting in the streets. I was born wise and superstitious: never blow a whistle
in hot afternoon sun, snakes will creep out the bushes to attack you.
I was born shoulders-steady, ready for unexpected burdens:
the biggest: I was born. I was born to our green and white flag,
booming music at 1:00 AM from the corner motel, yellowed-armpits
of teenage boys' shirts, pawpaw trees, crude oil, polluted water,
cassava farms, palm oil, plantains, six families to one bathroom.
I was born on the east edge of a canal, the wooden bridge across,
flimsy as our trust in government, driving us farther to the feet of faith.
We all—market women, lawyers, wife-beaters, adulterers, politicians,
drug addicts, housewives—were born as Nigeria, into churches, mosques,
shrines, synagogues, with one song on our lips, a prayer, a supplication:

May we not return the same way we came.

Diepreye

Diepreye is an Assistant Editor for *Michigan Quarterly Review*. She is the winner of a 2022 and 2023 *Academy of American Poets Prize*. Her poems are in or forthcoming with the *Academy of American Poets, Up the Staircase Quarterly, Rising Phoenix Press* and more.

Once, It Happened a Boy

It was in the liquid shade of a yucca tree
each quivering line of the boy's body broke

to silver, then leaf—
sharp contours assailing angled light

like a flotilla cutting waves, a vascular wing
macheteying

towards this clumsy shimmering
pool of soil

cradling my reflection like its own.
Once, it happened a boy.

It happened under over-ripened suns
at the pace of a fouling room—

his broke away from *mine*, left me
in this frame of mud and stone a canvas teetering

at the sharp edge of a new leaf, witness
to my own unfurling.

When I reached for him I dug out fists full
of wet hair, long stringy clumps flecked with ash,

gnats, tiny globular pellets like furry teeth
spat up from a pentimento world.

Crystal coronets of violet, indigo, cochineal
painted rings around my lips as I stayed up drinking

back the flowers of the yucca shade,
cupping my hands, *our* hands, to the blurring canvas

remembering the way an oil slick recalls the earth
the tilt of an August sky that held its blue

forever—once,
it happened a boy was made

the promise to be held the same: forever
in a breath of summer carried over coning lupine;

in a wonton splay of light
netting argosies

of dust, each fleck buoying a life
intent on surfacing,

no matter how or when or what
conditions of the surface

it happens—just that it happens,
the beauty you possess now on earth is seen, bright,

so unlike anything else.

Clayton Longstaff
Clayton Longstaff's work has appeared in publications that include *The Dalhousie Review*, *Geist*, *The Literary Review of Canada*, *Bending Genres*, *Prism* and elsewhere. He lives on the unceded traditional territory of the Lekwungen & WSÁNEĆ nations.

Portrait of My Father as a Postman

Your father is giving birth in the armchair.
He presses the beginnings of you together.
He pushes you out and wheels you round on his Royal Mail cart.
Build the world in letters! your father tells you;
and you will go on to conduct brutal interviews
instead of painting pictures when you grow up.

Twice your father left you out too long in the cold.
You clutched the red handles of his cart trying
to squeeze yourself warm, while he stuffed
all those metal mouths with sealed words.
When he finished you held out your curled fingers
and he put them in his hot wet mouth.
Later he tucked you under his arm like a special
delivery parcel and posited you home to a warm bath.

At the age of five your father advised you
on the emerging distance between your body and his body;
his nose skimming the small print of your birth certificate;
he took a bite of his toast, looked you up and down
and handed you a packet of second-class stamps.
He never spoke to you again after that.
For the longest time you turned yourself inside out
looking for paper cuts.

Your therapist asks, *what do you think memory does?*
and you tell her it's a stack of envelopes hungry for deliverance.
You tell her you have taken to sleeping in the arm-
chairs of strangers, that you had a lover once
who wheeled you around the Asda car park one night
as it snowed, and when you started to shiver
you thought you were in love.

Your therapist asks *what do you really remember?*
and you tell her about the chair you were born in,
your father's holy hands, how he uncurled you
like a prophecy and you uttered the first word.
Your therapist asks, *what happened next?*

And you inspect her office floor for the carpet stain
your father would have wax sealed in honour
of giving birth to you, right before he wheeled you out.

Sunnah Khan
Sunnah Khan is a Scottish Pakistani poet, creative facilitator & multidisciplinary artist. Her debut pamphlet *I Don't Know How To Forgive You When You Make No Apology For This Haunting* was published by Rough Trade Books (2020).

Prospect Park with My Mother During an Ectopic Pregnancy

/

She's traversed the Hudson:
unaccustomed juxtaposition.

When I'm well my complexities
scratch at her surface and she stays

in Jersey, longs for the tiny girl I was,
curls in 'tails, nose in books,

before I absconded to the loud side
of the river. Now the baby

must die so I can live. I didn't want to be a mother.
She wanted to be a grand/mother but not like this.

//

In these shadow-weeks, each
day may dawn my last. She's come

to witness the impending hemorrhage.
I'm sick, finally, and this she knows

how to get on with. No stories
from Rome or Taiwan, no book recommendations

to tax her scattered concentration, to remind her
she neither travels nor reads. Pregnant and dying,

eyes smoke and sunken, I look nothing
like the smack-talking kid she scolded after the rape,

It's the way you carry yourself.
He could smell it on you.

My mouth lacks the strength
for the twenty-year snarl I send her.

She simmers milk for my oatmeal,
shimmies my coat over my shoulders.

///

The doctors say walk,
but just a little. Blood must not pool,

must not rush. Orange gilds oaks,
particularly vibrant this year.

Red more rebellious. Every pace
a gift: felled-leaf fire curls

on concrete steps, the air's cool
with kisses. Every day we stroll

slow, so the dam won't burst.

Ivy Raff

Ivy Raff is the author of *Rooted and Reduced to Dust* (Finishing Line Press) and also *What Remains* (Editorial DALYA), winner of the *Alberola International Poetry Prize*. Her Best of the Net-nominated work has garnered support from the *Colgate Writers' Conference*.

Reflective Fragments Coated with a Thin Layer of Metal

Sadness is an oil stain on a nylon seat cover in a second-hand car
it asks irrelevant questions: *Why do supermarket flowers have no scent?*
and makes nonsensical statements:
Tribute bands are better than the real thing.

Tell me your name and I will see your colour
David is deep burgundy but if he is from Paris
and called Davide he is emerald green.

Sadness is not an oil stain: it is exhaust fumes.
There is no metaphor for happiness
that does not make me want to throw up.

Today I feel thaveless: a study showed that humans
need 4 hugs per day for survival and 8 for maintenance
so I should have died years ago or at least collapsed.

A cracked mirror in my bathroom reminded me of the wonder
of IKEA so I took it off the wall and dumped it in the black bin.
Carrie is an example of nominative determinism.

The Tarot predicts travel in my future: the airborne Eight of Wands
time to take a pilgrimage off the island
six years since my last flight. I am a stone or maybe an oak.

Even non-believers visit holy wells   tie ribbons on wishing hawthorns
walk the Camino   compare blisters on their heels
go home and evangelise Santiago. Some refuse to speak of it
if you ask why they will answer: *Go n-éirí an bóthar leat.*

f too can scream.

*thaveless: Ulster Scots meaning *lacking energy*
**Go n-éirí an bóthar leat*: Irish meaning *May your journey succeed*

Caroline Bracken

Caroline Bracken's poems have been published in *Gutter, The North, Poetry News, Poetry Wales* and elsewhere. Her poems have been shortlisted in the Manchester Poetry Prize and the Alpine Fellowship Prize. Recently, she has completed her debut poetry collection.

Song o' the River Itchen

My body knows the way to where I'm gwin,
has always know'd. I knows fen
and flooded meadow, kings and riots,
wet woodland, Saxons, swamp.
At Alresford, I quills up, gammocky,
hoops doun through Cheriton, bears a west
by way of Lovington, Ovington, Avington.
I knows what 'tis to hold: chock and otter,
pipe stem, doll's head, watercress.
At night, my veins run drunken with the moon.
I knows the damselfly's ticklun skitter,
the kingfisher's shot-blue flash agin' my banks,
the jack-hern's spellbound stance.
And I knows what 'tis to be held.
By Winchester,
I be but channelled,
a moated, tamed,
so I roars up a froth
that tumbles,
clockun, gloxun,
bluff through City Mill.
Summer evenuns, I drifts me easy
through The Weirs, blink bright with gold
past sun-warmed bricks o' disused wharves,
the flint rubble core o' Roman city walls.
After a while, I crosses the edgeland moors
at Winnall. Wintertimes, I sees
the brickle-limbed ghostés o' cow parsley,
pretty nigh froze in the act o' reachun.
At St Catherine's Hill, I be but smolt glass,
fleet, still. By Shawford, Twyford,
I be a speckle-back, writhun, brindled,
fit to burst my skin. Bubbles skate my surface
at Bittern: swimmy, glimmerun.
At last, I be drank in a wink by Solent seas:
quaffed as quick as empires be.

Tell it out. Time builds hisen borders
around everythun that lives.
Know what 'tis to be held by what you hold,
what 'tis to be held by what holds you.

Glossary of Hampshire words and phrases: *quill-up,* to rise as water does in a spring; *gammocky,* wild, full of tricks; *chock,* chalk; *jack hern,* a heron; *clockun,* the sound of falling water; *gloxun,* the music of gurgling water; *bluff,* lusty, like a farmer; *smolt,* polished, shining; *fleet,* a sheet of water; *speckle-back,* a snake; *brindled,* severe, fierce; *swimmy,* giddy in the head.

Kathryn Bevis

Kathryn Bevis's pamphlet, *Flamingo* (Seren), was one of the Poetry Society's Books of the Year (2022) and was shortlisted for the Saboteur Award for the Best Pamphlet (2022). Her debut collection, *The Butterfly House*, is due to be published by Seren in 2024.

SUNFRAIL

Table 9: information about your elderlies

90. number of cigarettes * (no longer applicable) * you should have seen her
in the sixties the photos my Father took hand on thigh/fag in hand
gorgeous

91. a) problematic alcohol consumption
describe) tonight I'll wash her off me with a shower and a nice glass of

b) problematic sugar or food consumption Friday is always Fish n' Chips
always always always
(describe) she picks off the batter for the seagulls the lawn aflight
green & white
flap-flap-snatchsnap

take your time / hurry up

92. lack of energy yes/no yes/ no/ (M)other – please specify
93. dizziness
94. a) prolonged morning stiffness* how can I be kinder? b) insomnia * how can I be kinder?
how can I c) chronic pain *be?

95. urinary incontinence fascinating Flip-Flo ease
96. faecal incontinence
97. constipation *take your time / hurry up*
if I get stuck behind a tractor the drive takes 35'
the wrong daughter
looks across the fields yearns taps
the steering wheel

~~98. allergies~~

99. concerns/anxiety I won't miss this/miss her/ will I?

100. glasses a) does not need would lose
b) needs, but does not have no no no
c) has, but does not use lost
d) uses loses *what?*

101. walking stick needs has (seven) but will she fucking use them?

102. "Have you experienced a memory decline in the past year?" *tell me again*
about your again
again

about your problematic

Rachel Goodman

Rachel Goodman's poems have featured in *The Alchemy Spoon*, *Magma* and many more. She was shortlisted for the Bridport Prize in 2017 and 2021. Her debut book, *Knee to Knee*, a collaboration with poet Elvire Roberts, will be published next year by *Dialect Press*.

Reticulum

the way grief moves through water/ the shape of your lips when they hole
the word *'whale'*/ my period-jumper that could take you under/ knot of a fist
that caught you out/ cells lined with lace sutured in code/ a head-dress with pin
curls for brains/ chiffon shaped to bait tiny sea-daughter pearls/ twinkles found
in the grounds of bête and film noir/ the rind of old eyes
punctured by love/   the way milk creeps   when spilt near a shoe/
the flare of things that eventually find you/ what the sky becomes
when it lands on black coffee and skin   that trawls/ trepanation/
the whisper of fontanelles/ herringbone gauze/ fishnets
on wetlegs writhing/ pink Meccano for girls/ blue macrame for boys/
maps with their A roads cut out/ a swarm of stars named www.

Reticulum in Latin means 'a little net' and was later given various uses in biology, cytology, histology, etc., and made a southern constellation by French astronomer, La Caille (1763).

Sujatha Menon
Sujatha Menon is a writer/artist and musician from the Midlands. Her poems have been published internationally and she is the author of *The Glass Puddle* (Vole) and *Night Swan to Nigg* (Cromarty Arts Trust). She is poet in residence at the University of Warwick.

Traces

Isaan, the vast rice-growing plateau in north-east Thailand

Endless paddies
stencil the land, enmesh the living.
Their waters smudge

a setting sun's inks. A hand
has wiped leftover pigments
on a cloth of sky.

A motorcycle
scratches the land
for epidermic dust, guessing

a low track, up to
a corrugated iron scar
of an outbuilding. What

pinprick of space is yours here?
The same as an old lady's,
squatting at a roadside. Your

boyhood world globe was a skin
encircling a lamp, which you spun
for all your tales to come. Now

you recall the rare times when,
dauntless, half-aware,
you tattooed the ready earth.

Christopher M James

Christopher M James, a dual British/French national, lives in the Dordogne, France. His work has been published in *Acumen*, *Dream Catcher* and *Poetry Salzburg* amongst others. He has won several competition prizes and runs the French Online Poetry Stanza.

The Cake Mixture

After Edip Cansever

a woman creams butter
and sugar in a mixing bowl

one, two, three yolks
and a tiny piece of shell

she adds the coldness
of milk and evening air

echoes of mothers
calling their children

the darkness in the room
she places in the bowl

conversations from her body
muffled like folded egg whites

loud edges of dreams
a French nursery rhyme

she makes a well and places
rubble from her mind

her shadow
counting each precious breath

she peers at the purple sky
drops an eclipse in the batter

the cake mixture puffs
sighs just a little

then a deafening calm
yet the woman keeps adding things.

Leah Larwood

Leah has an MA in Creative Writing from Birkbeck University. She is currently studying to be a gestalt psychotherapist and a certified poetry therapist. She has been widely published in a number of literary mags and has been placed in various prestigious competitions.

Vitrine

"A woman must continually watch herself. She is almost continually accompanied by her own image of herself."- John Berger

He showed you to your room in the gallery,
covered you in silver foil and placed you beneath
a heart and feather on scales, inside a vitrine.
You lacked privacy in the sunlight hours
when people would arrive as you breathed
against glass, drew pictures with your fingers
like a child on the window of a car. They watched,
trying to work you out, looking around for context,
because you came uncaptioned, although you realised
you had been highly curated when you could not open
the door from the inside. There were large pieces
of ripped cloth hanging from the gallery ceiling,
half-smoked cigars you could not smell, a young
boy's photograph and rusted bikes, coat hangers,
scraps of bark and iron filings. All of this you
could not touch. The scales stayed balanced.
Often you closed your eyes, avoiding the visitors.
You could not believe people had paid to see you.
You wondered how they saw you, what their brains
were saying, what they focused on about your clothes,
hair, the patterns you made. You decided, after three days,
to be cruel, to scratch on frightening phrases.
Their facial expressions changed, they stared less, moved
into other areas of the gallery, a section with windows,
a section that didn't sweat and piss when you peeled away
the foil, that didn't reflect the hidden parts of them.
From the scale you took the heart and it did not move.
From the scale you took the feather and it not move.
The artist never came to see what they had made.
When a week was over, the gallery manager let you leave
without any praise.

Georgia Conlon

Georgia Conlon is a poet, educator, and carnivore. Her work has been published in journals including *Obsessed with Pipework* and *The North*. She is the creator of *Georgia's Poetry Workshop* podcast and is completing her MA in Writing Poetry at Newcastle University.

Watching Reruns

1974
Sitting next to my father on the green velvet sofa watching
in glowing technicolor inside the wood framed oval screen
Spock is telling Captain Kirk it is illogical as Father
launches his whiskey-fueled sonic boom into the kitchen
why is dinner not on the table and bring me another
every evening he is home Mother braces for the next
Father always fires in salvos so I bury my face
every night into the pillow but still feel the boom
from his last detonation his fuel running low
as Mother steadies onto her feet her hands
pressed against the counter I can still hear
through the down the shot glass shatter
the ringing in my ears as shards of
tears hit the bruised linoleum floor—

2014
Sitting next to me on the brown leather sofa watching
in glowing digitally remastered color on the flat screen
Spock is telling Captain Kirk it is illogical as I look
into the kitchen the cooking timer chiming its rhythmic
tones into the living room and I say I think dinner is
ready as I rise to check and set the table this has been
our evening routine since her mother left too many
years ago my daughter now bounding to my side
saying Dad wait I want to help as we step through
the sliding glass door onto the patio passing
her freshly planted flower garden the sweet
scents of honeysuckle and rose swirling
whispers in the backyard breeze
rising to greet us at the grill—

AJ Baumely

AJ Baumel is a poet and teaching artist at the Virginia G. Piper Center for Creative Writing at Arizona State University and an instructor at the Osher Lifelong Learning Institute. He is a graduate of the Queens University of Charlotte MFA programme and a U.S. navy veteran.

Pass

After Nick Makoha

Pass (synonyms) **1.** *rid of waste: eliminate, evacuate* as in Eastern European pogroms which drove the family to leave home in search of lives without persecution. **2.** *move onward: leave, slip away* as in escape with only what can be carried—children, sewing machine, candlesticks. **3.** *permission: identification, safe-conduct* as in spend savings on forged passports, trade with traffickers—the overcoat for a winter boat passage. **4.** *express formally: declare, state* as in to speak of being stateless, lacking a homeland. **5.** *assimilate: blend in, overlook* as in adopt the culture of the new country and suppress heritage. **6.** *succeed: get through, meet required standard* as in unpick second hand clothes, remake into worker's garments, sell from a barrow, make clothes from new, sell in a shop, then several shops. **7.** *surpass: go beyond* as in expand into large scale manufacturing, become known for the iconic Lord Anthony snorkel parka coat. **8.** *decide not to do: omit, decline, forget* as in don't speak of the trauma, don't speak in the mother tongue, cover the mirror with silence. **9.** *opening through solid: cut* as in "split at the root", a disconnected third generation, a legacy of ghetto food and a few words accepted into the English language. **10.** *death:*

Kitty Martin

Kitty Martin has an MA in Writing Poetry from Poetry School / Newcastle University. She won Imtiaz Dharker's Chancellor's Poetry Prize (2022). Her poems have appeared in *NCLA*, *Poetry Salzburg* and *Tentacular,* amongst others. *Pass* was first published in *The North.*

What Insects Taught Me About My Mother

That you really can have eyes in the back of your head. That pretending to be what you are not – a twig, dead leaf, an orchid - is the best way to fend off predators. That there are advantages and disadvantages to being transparent. That it's okay not to have any maternal instinct; slinging offspring out of the nest as soon as they hatch, only encourages them to climb higher. That there is a good reason your kith and kin want to devour you whole. That if you coil up into an armoured jewel-like ball, you can't be hurt. That most parasites you try to rid yourself of will have thin waists. That happiness cannot be coaxed from artificial flowers however beautiful. That deprived of an opportunity to mate, common substitutes include sugar, nicotine, booze. That dancing in a figure of eight will always bring you home. That it's alright to yearn for the dark, to crawl into the cracks in the soil, to burrow under the loose bark of rotten trees to grieve.

Emjay

Emjay lives, walks and writes in the wilds of the North Pennines. She has won the Live Canon Poetry Pamphlet Prize, the Bath Novella-in-Flash Prize, the Bridport Poetry Prize and the Mslexia Flash Prize. She has been shortlisted for the Beverley International Prize.

When I was young they found a bat inside me

It must have flown in at night, my mouth agape like an unpicked pocket,
drawn the curtains of its wings around itself to glide down my windpipe

they need to hibernate from harsh winters, Google said,
the inside of me a settlement, a soft landing between two cages.

I hardly felt a presence at the start, only a gentle constriction in my
chest, at the back of the throat. But it grew there, in my torso, my life,

its wings expanding like root rot. The takeover was slow, they found me sleeping
in the day, writhing with insomnia at dawn. My body churned like butter.

In my pleural space this leathered creature lurked, each taking comfort
in the other's darkness. This bat, *my bat*, began to beat its wings, beating the

blue breath from me. When I woke I was propped up in a sterile room; yellow walls,
yellow lights, yellow faces. *The bat has gone*, the doctor said, *you should feel*

much better now. Everyone looked so relieved. But I was hollowed, an abandoned
trench with only a vague sense of what it once sheltered.

An endoscopy confirmed it, nothing, not a trace.
Just tissues, organs and shocking, shocking light

Caroline Druitt

Caroline is a poet and teacher. Her poems have been published by *AndOtherPoems*, *Lucent Dreaming*, *The North*, commissioned by Apples and Snakes, long-listed for the Outspoken prize, shortlisted for the Bridport Prize and commended in the National Poetry Competition.

Word Problems for Ten Marks Each

(after Bhaskara II's 'Lilavati')

1. If, on a full moon night,
a boy, nineteen, climbs all forty-four steps
to flat B-205 and leaves
without getting my brother's number,
how many suns will it take
to feed courage to his feet again?

2. If Firuza, of the straight A's
and curved waist, who has learned
to clasp her chemistry books to her chest,
is the regular source of optical data
to five pairs of unblinking, pursuant eyes,
how many weeks before her father
decides she doesn't
need college anymore?

3. If Tap A can fill three buckets in a minute
and Tap B can fill half a bucket,
if Tap A is molded from ancient brass
and Tap B from mongrel alloy,
if Tap A belongs to the fourth bathroom of a bungalow
and Tap B to a cracked gas station basin,
what will the astrologer need to be paid
to see alignment in their stars?

4. If one two-armed man
can build half a wall in eight days
and one two-armed woman
can build three quarters of a wall in a dozen days,
how many walls will need to fall
before they hold the same number
of two-faced coins in their two hands?

5. *(Bonus Question)*
If Hari, who washes your car,
has to divide seven rotis and two onions
between five children,
explain why
Hari, who washes your car,
has to divide seven rotis and two onions
between five children.

Pervin Saket

Pervin Saket is Poetry Editor of *The Bombay Literary Magazine* and is also the cofounder of the Kolam Writers' Workshop. In 2021, she was awarded the Srinivas Rayaprol Poetry Prize. She is curator for Literature at the Kala Ghoda Arts Festival in Mumbai, India.

Mother Crow, Mother Bee, Mother Stone, Mother Sky, Mother Tree

I had a mother once. I called her *Crow*   for the way she perched
  her voice upon her tongue   *Crow* for the way her songs
 seemed full of early morning pain   *Crow* for her oil-shine curls
 for words shaped like hollow bone   for claws

I called her *Bee*   for the way she worked her garden, knee-deep
in flowers, plucking out dead faces   *Bee* for every sting. *Bee*
for the thought of honey in the stoppered tomb   of her heart
  I looked at my mother   at how she stood

as if each bone must accept the burden   of the other bone above
  I called her *Stone*   for the way her throat was a cold church
 Stone for the skinned hill of each collarbone, *Stone*   for the slab
  of her sleeping back, forever turned against

I called her *Sky*   for the way she hung her weight over my head
Sky for the shadow, blue from eyelid to brow   *Sky*
for the way she believed in angels   I remember how her lips
were like the edges of a broken cup   I felt how much

  she did not want to be touched. She said   *you children*
will be the death of me   *I had a daughter once*   she said
  I called her Sea   *Daughter made from storm and salt*
   Sea for sickness, for drowning

 I threw her my love   it rattled like a pebble down a well
  I had a daughter once   she said   *I called her Wrong*
for the way she was not thin or good   *Wrong for the way*
she was made   *Daughter*   *built from accidents*

I had a mother once. I called her *Tree*   for the way I hung
  from her arm like a leaf   the way I was shaken lose   *Tree*
 for the way I fell at her feet   *Tree* for the length of the shadow
  she cast   for the sun she tried to carry upon her crown

Jane Burn

Jane Burn is a working-class, pansexual, essayist, poet, artist and person with autism. Her work has been widely published and anthologised. she has an MA in Writing Poetry from Newcastle University. Her latest collection, *Be Feared,* is available from Nine Arches Press.

Ocean Pastoral with Bedroom

Caracas 2023

what would change if American Literature included the literature of American imperialism and warfare, no matter where it was written from?
—Amy E. Elkins

darling boy, your eyes are clouding white again — the damp in here
is rotting them. let's open the windows. give me
a smile. tell me how your fist hit the concrete hard enough to open into a hand,
we're going to go to a special report now
say "I love you", because you cannot muster "forgive me".
from abc news.
try to say it as I clutch on to your throat,
the same desperate way a man holds a buoy, with the black sea turning
blacker in his ears. I push down to stay afloat. you close your eyes.
say it, & smile: a flash of your teeth, curved & glinting like a distant
machete, now move close to me faster than the little seconds can leave: show me
all of your hands. tell me that shore is just another way of saying certainty.
we're joined here by the entire abc network.
say "love", again. say it with your eyes sealed tight as a letter
from a distant country. say "love" in lieu of "forgive me", again. darling
good morning america was in progress but
this is how it begins: you're panting,
your mess of blonde hair is shaped like ten-thousand men
all heaped & curled up with exhaustion, begging
we have received some breaking news.
you to love me tenderly, as you bite down on the word to make it sharp,
and smile, sweating. say "love", & say it quickly.
your teeth white as lily petals, peeling away into the mid-dark.
it is 8:52 a.m. here &
say you "love this country"
(as another red dawn fades), but say it
with wild blue eyes, like a threat, say it like all
good americans.
say it as you fall.

we are receiving some breaking news from new york
say "love" one last time, my hands tightening around your perfect neck.
say "love", as if the word alone will save you.
there is one report, as of yet unconfirmed,
that a plane has hit the world trade centre.
& kiss me goodbye.

Armando Ledezma
Armando Ledezma is a Venezuelan-British poet based in London. He is currently studying for a Master's Degree in Creative Writing at the University of Oxford. He was awarded the *Les Arnold Prize for Poetry*. His poems have appeared in journals online and in print.

FICTION

What an immense pleasure it has been to participate in the Aesthetica Creative Writing Awards. As judges for the Short Fiction panel we have been able to read a vast range of entries and have had to go through a difficult process in selecting the most deserving anthology pieces. All of the works were strong and memorable in their own ways and would be named if the word count allowed. Sadly, only twenty were able to make the final cut for publication from hundreds of entries.

As in previous years, the panel draws on expertise from all areas of the literary world: publishing, literary agencies, cultural historians, literary linguists, writers and the teachers of creative writing. Richard Price, Emma Newport, Susmita Bhattacharya, Ansa Khan Khattack, Aliya Gulamani, Sabhbh Curran, Sofia Akel, Alfonzo Sieveking and myself brought all of our experience alongside our passion and enthusiasm to the task at hand. After much discussion we were unanimous in agreeing that the selected stories are truly representational of new writing.

Some of the themes this year ranged from climate change, domestic physical abuse and suicide through to race and dystopic fiction, combining brilliant writing with emotional delivery taking the reader on multiple journeys. *Helen Jo* and *Unleashed* are both stories that foreground real control over the prose and contain emotional depth. *Helen Jo*'s compelling portrait of a mother that was at times kind of grotesque, but also deeply heartfelt, with a real sense of frustration, was extremely compelling. *Unleashed* has emotional complexity and intergenerational tensions, bordering on a body horror. *Say Hello to Yamma* achieves a lot given the limited word count. A very dense and complex story enables the reader to reflect on the impacts of climate change on small communities. *Sweetheart*, *Certificate of Infertility*, *Doreen's Last Day*, *In the Face Of(f)* and *Will you DSM me?* transport readers into different worlds and mindsets. These stories are creatively constructed, tackling difficult and emotive topics in a sensitive manner.

Mothering, family and other relationships are recurrent themes evidenced in *Mother Love*, *Footsteps of my dear mother*, *Covenants Considered*, *Some Life* , *This* and *The Daily Walk*. Intriguingly, *Two Children with a Book*, has a semiotic approach, where the reader attempts to imagine the lives of the story's sitting girls within a rare portrait. Elsewhere, *Betty Crocker Directs the Test Kitchen to Submerge* reveals complex American tensions, observing history, race and enslavement from an unexpected perspective. *A little slice of suburban American life*, alongside some unlikeable characters, has the ability to invoke empathy and questions about American history. Much like all of the stories in our shortlist, *Taking out the Trash* and *Does the Wind blow colder at home?* exemplifies the brilliant writing executed by the authors of this year's successful entries.

The overall winner stood out almost from the beginning of our deliberations. Our initial discussions in selecting first place involved three excitingly compelling stories: *Mr Street*, *Saltbush* and *Birdie*. *Birdie* tells the story of domestic physical abuse. It's told cleverly through the words of one child, who adopts aggressive and explicit language. The voice and tone used is very effective. *Saltbush* is in a completely different genre. It is a dystopic work about the desert taking over and the issue of the dust coming into town. Strange and atmospheric, the reader doesn't quite know where the story is going, as an extra layer of mystery is added. *Saltbush* has a lyrical complexity, density and quality that makes it stand out. It is a sophisticated piece of writing that rewards re-reading and contemplation as it reflects on the climate crisis in Australia. Our overall winner, however, is *Mr Street*. *Mr Street* is a surprising portrait of a male teacher who exposes himself to his female students. It is framed in a unique way. It is fantastically written: the voice is brilliant and the story has a high concept which is delivered well. The opening sequence has the reader anticipating a particular direction for the story which is never realised. The female students are compassionate and understanding. They know what is happening and become protective of the teacher.

As a panel we really valued the elements in the short fiction entries that made us want to revisit these stories. Concept, control, emotional delivery, poetics and plot and sophisticated writing are just some of the ingredients that create a great piece of fiction.

Dr Marl'ene Edwin
Chair, Short Fiction Prize,
Aesthetica Creative Writing Award

Dr Marl'ene Edwin is Deputy Director at the Centre for Caribbean and Diaspora Studies & Senior Fellow of the HEA and Churchill Fellow. Her research includes Caribbean Creole Languages and Oral Literature. She convenes the module Literature of the Caribbean and its Diasporas.

WINNING ENTRY

Mr Street

We first had a sense of something awry when Mr Street said *Cunt* unexpectedly during registration. Amra was sitting in the front row and was sure it was directed at her.

But at the back it felt more general, spoken to all of us, about all of us. We were girls after all and fourteen-year-olds. We'd long suspected he struggled with us; our newly curvy bodies seemed to give him unease. We were creatures undergoing transformation with softness in unfamiliar places. We breathed hormones and trickiness. Where were the little sticklike tots we were yesterday, all leggy and thin? Where had the teeny bambinis gone? The little yearlings?

He was easily discomfited, and like Pavlov's dog, he spluttered with Amra's *Sir, Sir, can you explain what is meant by 'intercourse'?* and he'd be off, unable to get a sentence out, sometimes not even a word.

But today was different. He said *Cunt*, stared into space, then said *Dick Fuck Cunt Cunt Cunt*, in quick succession, followed by a weird snickering laugh.

We just sat there watching the horror show unfold. It was still only nine in the morning.

He started to untie his tie and stripped it off from round his neck, rolled it up and put it in his pocket, then he unbuttoned his shirt, a striped one, and pulled it off, over his head. He looked a bit sweaty, and his hair was now sticking up, and he stood there at the front of the classroom with no top on, in the buff but not buff if you know what I mean, carefully shaking out and folding his shirt, and draping it over the back of a chair. His chest was pink with pale hairs, a body that's never seen sunlight.

When he started to undo his belt, we knew we had to stop him. At least some of us. Amra, our leader, said *Sir, Sir, don't do that.* But he just carried on, coiling up his belt and putting it neatly on his desk.

Rachel was drawing a cartoon titled *Half Naked Mr Street* for Farzana and Erica who were prodding her with *Quick Rach, Quick, Get it all down, Get the detail.* Rachel crossed out *Half* and sat back to watch as he went for his trousers. Lorna was holding her fingers up in a pretend camera square. Beatrice said, *Let the show go on, let him get buck naked.* He let his trousers drop and started to step out of them, getting stuck with trying to undo his shoelaces. His underpants were boxers, luckily. Maroon Calvin Kleins from TK Maxx or somewhere.

But what we all saw were the marks, and we knew these very well, identical to our own in different stages of healing.

Rachel stopped drawing as we stared at the finely drawn horizontal cuts lacing ladder-like up Mr Street's thighs, the march of the razor, self-inflicted and very much not for public view.

A momentary religious hush.

Then Amra shouted *SIR! SIR! What are you doing!?* Getting up and almost pushing her desk over as she tried to get his attention. Then high pitched, almost a scream, *SIR!* And he came round and suddenly seemed to see us.
Sir, you need to get dressed.

He took immediate stock of the bad situation and pulled his trousers up, which did take quite a long time, as he was in a bit of a tangle. But he did get straight, and also found his shirt which he pulled over his head, and his belt from the desk, and the tie from his pocket. His fingers were a bit trembly. We were all watching. He had no idea how relieved we were as he tucked in his shirt and fastened his belt. He just stood there looking devastated. And flushed.

The bell went. End of registration. We filed out in awkward silence.

We felt sad. As if something had been broken.

We walked to our lessons, as the whispering started up and scattered round school.

If nuclear fallout had a sound, this was it. A quiet hissing and fizz, while its poisonous dust was getting into all the corners. Tiny tiny corrosive fragments, missives, whispered and rustling, settling like toxic confetti. Was it us saying these things? That Mr Street took his clothes off, that he has a nipple ring, a sleeve tattoo of a demonic bird, that he is covered in a depiction of the Virgin Mary with her legs splayed open, that his pubic hair is ginger, that his penis is pierced. That it was erect, *Standing to Attention.* That he has rippling muscles. That he stood naked, jutting his hip out, curling a beckoning finger, *Come and get it, Girls.*
Apparently, he pissed in the stationary cupboard.

We saw him leaving school early, through the gates with his rucksack, the walk of shame.
We thought about him waiting at the bus stop alone and then faltering onto an empty bus. So tall but always tripping over. Maybe he dropped his glasses and had to pick them up. We weren't there to pick them up for him. *There you are Sir, blind as a bat, old as a mole, silly as a filly. We know you're not that old Sir, we know you're like thirty or forty or something, just jesting Sir.*

The day went on and nothing else was talked about all across school. Except no one mentioned those horizontal scars up his leg.

At home our mothers and fathers asked us about it in quiet voices. All over town they were talking to each other, on the phone or in each other's houses, trying to corral the information. They were careful with us. Were we upset? We must be traumatised.

So, what *exactly* went on?

Tell me *exactly.*

Did he touch you?

Did he touch any of you?

What did he do? What exactly happened?

Holly's mum says she said…

> *Holly isn't in our class. She doesn't have Mr Street.*
> *We're tired, please leave us alone.*
> *We are feeling sick*
> *We want to go to bed.*

In bed we speak on our phones, the inner circle, those who were there, hushed and under the sheets. Erica says *It is epilepsy like a fit, that's what he had.* Farzana says *It's Tourette's when you can't stop your body from doing things.* Lorna says *Shelly Murphy's little sister has that, she blinks over and over. Shelly says she can't control it.* Leah says *He keeps tablets in his satchel. We saw them, remember?* Rachel says *You don't take tablets for Tourette's. They don't work for it.* Bini says *Maybe he's a sex predator and the tablets are to stop his impulses.* Amra says *It wasn't sexual, he was undressing like a man who lives alone and folds up his clothes.* Sadia says, *how would you know Amra?* Beatrice says, *well, whatever, he might get the sack now.*

And we all think about this.

Mr Street is tall and thin, kind of elongated, and not fanciable, we have no idea of his personal life, he doesn't have a wedding ring, he wears an old-fashioned wind-up watch not a fitness tracker. He is not blokey like Mr Pearce and isn't shagging Kris the secretary like we know Mr Hayter is. Mr Hayter's daughters used to go to our school. Apparently, he shags Kris in her office after school. Amra's little brother saw him when he went back into school to get his fleece. They were on all fours, and he was doing it to her from behind. That's called *Doggy Style.* Mr Street isn't like that, he reads books and catches the bus. He's not a jogger like Mr Sandy with his weird twisty run. He's not a creep like Mr McKenzie who told

Amra she has beautiful hair and stroked it between his fingers.

Mr Street tells us what we need to know, and makes bad jokes, but we like him, he is kind of breakable, like he's been put together a bit wrong. We have been setting him up on a dating app, and he seems to like this, we have written his profile for him, with a photo that Lorna found of him online, and we told him he's got lots of interest already. We have created a perfect match for him, someone called Ada Lovebird, and she likes travel, sketching and reading and is single and looking for love and marriage. We have rewritten her a few times. She's gone from being sexually experienced to being a virgin and back again, and her piercings vary.

He knows us, knows which ones of us eat and which ones don't, he knows if we are sad or happy and who is sad and who is happy and what our parents are like, if they are rubbish or not, and he can sense if we have had breakfast. He reads us out the news, and makes us talk about current affairs, though he knows we want affairs of the heart. *Please Sir, tell us, are you in love? What's she called, can we have her number, so we can tell her all about you, because you are shy, and you won't do a proper job. Where did you meet her?*

Mr Street has a sketch pad in his satchel, we found it once when he left the classroom to get photocopying paper and we went through it just because we could. It was the time Beatrice touched a dead banana and got it on her hands. Leah says that was the time we saw the tablets. The dead banana time.

The next day Mr Street isn't here. And it is different in our classroom, like the light won't switch on properly. A cover teacher Mrs Frost arrives and sits down in Mr Street's chair and doesn't say one word to us for the whole of registration. Rachel circulates a tiny bit of paper, with *cold bitch by name cold bitch by nature* and a very good drawing of Mrs Frost with her mean lips and over-plucked eyebrows.

We don't say anything out loud to each other. It's safer. But we know what we all think, like how trees communicate bad news to each other underground, what to avoid, and who might bring disease.

During first period, Amra is called to the Headmistress's office. We watch Amra stand, gather her things as if she might be a while, then she changes her mind and leaves her coat and all her stuff, and goes out with nothing, like she won't be gone long. She shuts the door after her. We all watch the door.

Mrs Shipstone is our Headmistress. We named her *The Royal Yacht Britannia* but usually just call her *The Ship*. *The Ship* is huge. Leah said maybe the school governors will smash a bottle of champagne on her backside when she retires, as a send-off.

Amra comes back after about twenty minutes, then Rachel is called. Rachel is gone only a few minutes. Then it is Farzana, then Lorna, then Leah, then Erica, Beatrice, Bini and Sadia.

The Ship gets us in one by one and asks *What Happened Yesterday. At Registration?*

And we say *Nothing Miss, what do you mean?*

Don't know what you are talking about.

Those stories aren't true.

We were there and nothing happened.

Mr Street was normal to us, Miss, he's always normal.

Mr Street is the most normal person Miss. He's Mint.

We did hear the gossip, but it isn't true, we don't think Mr Street has any tattoos, maybe you could check.

The next day, Mr Street is back. Standing at the front of the classroom trying to assemble paper handouts but struggling with the stapler. A bit trembly but that's normal.

He does looks neater and tidied up though. Brushed. Haircutted. Like he's been ironed. Flattened.

He still has his satchel so that's a good sign.

Hi Mr Street, glad you're here Sir.
Had a good break Sir?
We missed you Sir.
There's no one like you, Sir. We told The Ship that you're Mint.
We didn't like the cover teacher Sir. She ignored us.

Lucy Campbell

Lucy Campbell is a writer, filmmaker and doctor based in Manchester, UK. Her short films have been funded by BFI, Film4, BBC Films and have won multiple international awards. She is known for sci-fi dramas *Pig Child* and *Marina & Adrienne*.

The Daily Walk

There was a nice quiet neighborhood tucked away in the heart of the city. This neighborhood had very little crime to speak of. The neighborhood had a mix of people of all ages and from all walks of life. Although it was surrounded on all four sides by busy roadways, it was of little consequence since it had sidewalks and bike trails that bordered the streets. During various times of the early morning hours one can see elderly couples going for a morning walk, moms jogging with their strollers, and people walking various breeds of dogs, both big and small. In the evening, the same array of activities can be seen only done by a different shift. Kids would ride their bikes, play at the park with their friends, or swim at the pool during the summer. A lake was at the center of the neighborhood where men would go fishing with their boys, or parents and their children would feed the waterfowls bread and crumbs. Oh yes, this neighborhood certainly harkened back to the days of the 80s and 90s.

In this neighborhood there were to men, Mr. White and Mr. Black who had very much in common. While one lived close to one entrance of the neighborhood, the other lived on the opposite end near the other entrance. they were both Veterans of the Desert Storm Iraq War. Both men had been retired for less than five years and were still adjusting to their new way of life. They were both exactly the same age to the point that they shared the same birthday. There are many other commonalities the two would discover should they ever have a conversation. In fact, their morning routines were nearly identical. In the morning they both would wake up, thank God for another day, stretch, and then put on a cup of coffee while they made their beds. They would then go outside while still wearing a robe or pajamas to retrieve the morning paper. Next, they would sit at their kitchen tables and drink their coffee while reading the paper. After this they would brush their teeth and put on their walking attire. Finally, they would open all of the curtains and blinds that they desired to let the light in for the day. If one day these two should ever meet, they would no doubt fast become best friends.

Now they were ready for the best part of their morning routine... "The Walk". The two men set off from their homes and trotted in the opposite direction. They would enjoy the fresh air, scenery, and cardio. They would walk until they were both on the same sidewalk heading in different directions. They would soon look up and notice each other. Mr. Black cleared his throat and prepared to say "good morning" to Mr. White. Mr. White looked over his shoulder and then ahead to make sure there were no cars approaching. Before Mr. Black could speak, Mr. White crossed over the double laned divided street on to the other side. Mr. Black did not think much of it as Mr. White could have very well crossed over to get to his destination. After several paces, Mr. Black curiously looks back over his shoulder to see that Mr. White had crossed back over to his original side.

The next day was no different. Both men woke up, conducted their normal routines, and then went for a walk. Once again, they would meet as the loop around the neighborhood would guide them to do so. This time the men noticed each other at an even greater distance than the previous day. Mr. Black once again cleared his throat and prepared to say good morning. Mr. White looked over his shoulder and then in front of him. Once no cars were coming, he crossed the street at an even further distance than the previous day. Mr. Black, thinking that it may be a coincidence, looks over his shoulder to see that Mr. White has again crossed back over to his original side.

The next day both men conducted their normal routines but with slight deviations. Mr. Black and Mr. White both altered and dragged out their daily goings in an attempt to avoid the unpleasantness of the other man ruining their walks. While walking, both men were surprised to see that they both had delayed their routines about the same amount of time. The loop had again brought them on a course to pass each other in opposite directions. Mr. White looked over his shoulder to make sure the way was clear. When he looked ahead, he saw that Mr. Black had started crossing the street before he could. Once across the street, Mr. Black looked over to see that Mr. White stayed on his original side and did not cross the street. Mr. Black crossed back over to his original side. Neither man looked over their shoulders and they finished their walks.

This day both men reverted back to their original morning routines and set out for their walks. The loop brought them around and Mr. White walked towards Mr. Black until he realized that Mr. Black was not going to cross the street. Mr. Black cleared his throat and prepared to say, "good morning." He looked up and saw Mr. White crossing the street. From that day forward, Mr. Black did not try to cross the street before Mr. White, but Mr. White would do so every time. This routine went on for months.

One night there was a terrible thunderstorm. As Mr. White and Mr. Black settled into their beds, they could only hope that the rain would stop by morning. When they awoke, they were pleased to see that the rain had indeed stopped. It was a beautiful morning, and the sun was shining on both men's houses as they progressed through their routines. Meanwhile, across town there was a third man named Mr. Bad, who was up to no good.

Mr. Bad had very little routine in his life. Mr. Bad preferred spontaneity over schedule and he cared little for others. This particular morning Mr. Bad decided to rob a bank. After armed robbing the bank teller, he made his way to his lifted truck and sped away. However, it wasn't before long that the police were hot on his tail.

Back in the neighborhood, Mr. Black and Mr. White had opened up the curtains in their houses and set out for a walk. As they walked the neighborhood loop, they noticed that the ground was still wet, but the pavement had been dried by the morning sun. They also noticed several downed branches, leaves, and other debris scattered about by last night's thunderstorm. They were still able to appreciate the freshness in the air after the rain.

As Mr. White and Mr. Black became closer to passing each other on the loop, they both heard sirens in the distance. Mr. Bad was leading a high-speed chase directly to their neighborhood. On the street where Mr. Black and Mr. White usually pass, there was a tree that had been knocked down by the storm and was blocking the road. City workers were moving as quickly as they could to remove the tree, as traffic was beginning to pile up.

Both men noticed the unusual excitement as they neared each other. Mr. Black clears his throat and prepares to speak to Mr. White regarding last night's storm or the road blockage. Mr. White checks his clearance and begins to cross the street. As Mr. White crosses, Mr. Bad skids around the corner and floors it toward the roadblock. Mr. Bad was still closely pursued by the police, so he did not slam on the breaks. Instead, Mr. Bad jumped over the median with his truck and landed on the opposite side. Mr. Bad did not see Mr. White crossing the street as he was concealed by the blockage. Therefore, Mr. Bad struck Mr. White with his truck sending him flying through the air. Mr. White flew back across the street and landed on the sidewalk directly in front of Mr. Black. Mr. Black looks down at Mr. White, clears his throat, and says "Good morning."

David Hudson

David Hudson has written stories since he was a kid. He appreciates the freedom in creativity that comes with writing fiction. He would one day like to become a successful book author and screenwriter. He is in the process of fine tuning his craft.

Betty Crocker Directs the Test Kitchen to Submerge

After her divorce, E. would often tell people that hosting the dinner party with recipes from the vintage cookbook seemed harmless, like charades or a costume party. On a Saturday in July, E. was storing seasonal yard decorations in the attic when she noticed the 1964 *Betty Crocker* cookbook outside the bin containing her mother's last household. She'd moved Lidia to assisted living when it was still muddy outside. Lidia had been unusual in their town in Vermont in the early 1980s--a woman from Poland who worked as a bank teller, E.'s father a mystery. Occasionally, Lidia met a decent man with a cardigan tied around his throat, but those relationships ended for undramatic reasons, and E. wouldn't see her mother's boyfriend again.

The attic was airless. In the July heat, a trapped finch moldered between a windowpane. Fetally curled wasps were scattered on the unfinished floor. Several stories below, a lawn mower suddenly cut off. As E. returned the cookbook to the storage bin, she saw the spears of the feather duster in a nest of ratty dish towels smelling of old cooking butter. Rick had given her the feather duster as a gag gift after her promotion at Delco. Under the feather duster, she found the cheese knife engraved with a line from Wallace Stevens, so tarnished the knife could be a rock from another planet. E. hadn't written a poem in years. Near the top of her field, E. was discussed as a candidate for executive director of the national organization because of her reputation for anticipating the aftermath of employee decisions. She began flipping through recipes for Lobster Thermidor and a Moss Ball. With interest, she read about melting butter for a Noodle Ring and softening gelatin for a Ham Mousse. *What a lark*! Green Peas in a Rutabaga Nest, Pork Chops Supreme, Seafood Newburg, Hawaiian Sweet Balls, Chicken a la King.

E. could picture her guests milling around the kitchen island—Diana still in a conservative suit, Monique, and Charlotte—pinching wine glass stems and sharing a good laugh at the cookbook illustrations of bullet-breasted housewives, sampling dishes of a long-faded American lifestyle from an ironic distance. The attic was airless.

For nearly seven years, the first Friday of the month, the quartet of friends had met for dinner through job changes, relocation, a house fire, miscarriages, slow decline of elderly parents, one and a half divorces, a diagnosis, and Diana voting for the opposite political party. Normally, it was just bring a bottle of wine of goodwill or an appetizer of casualness. E. had marveled how the friendships had endured personal triumphs without a quarantine of the successful and with minimal groupthink. After Diana corrected, Actually, she was voting for the other candidate, dessert spoons were abandoned in the excavated slopes of kiwi tart slices, but the following month the dinner group gathered, and again after

Charlotte inadvertently caused the overdose of her neighbor's stepson, a real pest. The boy pushed his hand past the blooming white lilac to reach Charlotte's prescription on the ground floor bathroom sill and greeted death with cold etiquette.

That Friday E. clicked off CNN yammering in the family room and turned off NPR on the kitchen sound system. The kitchen filled with an afternoon sunlight she was so rarely home to witness. She unwrapped another onion and moved closer to the cookbook on the pewter stand. E.'s oversized house acquired a new room with the stenciled Test Kitchen of Scandinavia, its blue and white crockery and sweeping fjord taped on the window, followed by the wood-paneled Test Kitchen of Japan, sealed off from the world like a sauna, a picture of a blossoming cherry tree on the window. Two employees in A-line dresses and beehive hairdos lathed frosting onto a practice run of cakes; two businessmen in copycat thin ties scooped cocktail peanuts from a bowl.

On the stone walkway that evening, past the sapling with landscaping tag rattling in the breeze, each guest cradled a covered dish based on a recipe E. had emailed. Charlotte slipped in her mules. Diana locked her dull gold Audi with her hand not carrying the salad bowl. On page 76, the two businessmen in thin ties and carrying briefcases stepped up the walkway past a young maple tree. Any second now, they'll open the foyer door, the alpha male announcing, "Let's see what the wife's fixing for dinner." "Why we're not living in one of those Asian countries, are we, girls?" E. trilled in a pistachio green cocktail dress and matching cardigan when her guests removed their shoes. Charlotte and Monique exchanged looks.

In the vault of a living room, a retro coffee table held hors d'oeuvre of the unfamiliar—a Moss Ball, Smoked Egg Dip, Bambinos, Cocktail Buns, Vienna Sausages, and *Gwah-ka-mo-lay*; a Hollywood Dunk, canapé tray, and Liverwurst Pate. Charlotte and Monique craned appetizers onto napkins. "You've outdone yourself" and "However did you find the time" in voices beginning to sound like radio and tv announcers from another era.

When E. escorted them to the dining room, the table was set with Melmac dishware and laden with items from the special menu section—Eisenhower's Enjoy Life on Gettysburg Farm, United Nations Leader Chooses Dinner Favorite of Many Men, Glamour Surrounds Simple Supper of Famous Opera Star, Election Night at Home, and Fashion Luncheon. E.'s guests ate cautiously from the endless food, not at all their hostess' usual Cooking Channel cuisine. It was the aftertaste that had lingered in their mothers' mouths from casseroles served when they were brought home to meet their husband-to-be's parents, or the flavors that coated their grandmother's palates, remarks withheld. Their own rights and desires were as unnecessary as parsley. It was mixing carefully as directed. It was not upsetting the cart, not appearing driven. There was no Human Resources. They were without the E.R.A. How was this possible? It was spoonsful of campaigns ending in a man elected. What are your clerical skills? It was leaving your job once you had something in the oven.

They ate in resignation, except for Monique, who lifted her head while the pack kept drinking at the watering hole. Monique glanced at E. sipping her Grasshopper at the head of the table. The group chewed and swallowed with only a brief respite when E. pulled a Yale Law sweatshirt over her green dress.

By the time they reached dessert, a reasonable chiffon cake, it was nothing they could politely decline. Cakes are trademark Betty Crocker. Each guest was force fed a message, layer by layer. It was the assassination of confidence, the first course in a life with d-e-l-i-t-e from the sides of boxes and bottles, not in their bodies. The cake of suffocating niceness. They admired E.'s manicure as she held the door because the "Hints for Homemakers" Section advised, to "Refresh your spirits. Before breakfast, comb hair, apply makeup and a dash of cologne. Does wonders for your morale and for your family's, too!"—E. waving like a First Lady or an airline stewardess and everyone waving back, except Monique.

****

A month later, E. volunteered to host because the contractor was behind remodeling Charlotte's kitchen. The week of the Friday get-together, E. spotted the *Deerwood Cookbook* on her daughter's rug, next to a St. Lyon's Prep field hockey uniform. The last time E.'d seen the *Deerwood Cookbook* was at a rich girl's off-campus apartment, a sophomore who could buy bulky sweaters and silver jewelry from South American venders in the campus center. E. sent invitations on paper bags--arrive whenever they wanted after five, and could they bring a bottle of wine.

"I hope you're ready to cook," E. wearing an Indian print skirt and peasant blouse, barefoot, toenails unpainted. Monique put a finger to her grandmother's butterfly brooch, Charlotte to the top button of a vintage sweater. An electric fondue kit and a Crock Pot, a Mr. Coffee maker in mustard yellow and avocado green crowded the chrome espresso maker. The guests rolled up their sleeves to make Gypsy Soup, Chilled Beet Borsch, Bulgarian Pepper Casserole, polenta pie, eggplant curry, and Mushroom Moussaka while drinking jam glasses of wine from a jug.

It was the patchouli of not seeking approval, of margins loosened. It was freedom from "letting herself go." It was nothing exactly measured, everything bought in bulk. After dinner, roughly hewn carob brownies were served with mugs of mint tea. Diana and Monique argued about whether the ERA ever passed.

Everyone returned to their abodes relaxed with friendship and with leftovers in yoghurt containers, except Charlotte. When Diana splashed soy sauce on her dress, Charlotte fumed, Who didn't keep stain remover in her laundry room?

Diana's mother had entered hospice, so E. offered to host. On Google Books, she downloaded Eliza Jameson's 1854 *Miss Jameson's Complete Cookery in Its Various Branches,* the cookbook the Lincolns brought to the White House. A Goose Pie. Roast Woodcock or Plover with a Lobster or Nasturtium Sauce, served with Potato Snow and Indian Corn. Complaints are incessant about the deterioration of the servant class, but may not this growing evil be traced to the deterioration of the mistresses in the practice of a well-ordered household? E.'s daughter Madison is at an Honors Society retreat, or was it field hockey camp? In buying calves feet for jelly, procure those that have been singed and not skinned. In choosing fresh fish, select those with bright scales, the gills a lively red and the eyes prominent. Her fish monger wasn't at the market; instead, a sullen pimply girl took forever to pile cod on the scale. On the day of the party, E. rose at 4 AM to turn on the stove, as it will take a good part of the morning for the oven to reach temperature. She scoured surfaces with vinegar with newspaper, calling occasionally to the hired girl who didn't answer.

"You are likely the first persons to taste this soup in over a hundred years, prepared as it is from dried cod, potatoes, pork belly, and black pepper from India." The three women listened from embroidered chairs. The chowder floated in oils as though they were picnicking inside a crypt in the rain. A day would arrive when their diplomas and certificates would be tugged from frames. For Diana, the soup recalled a petrified duck egg given to her by a journalist who'd been at Tiananmen Square. Monique thought it likely that the chowder had last been prepared by enslaved sisters. The guests accepted a slice of Federal Cake, wishing for a private driver for the weary ride home. In the foyer, E. decided she might call on Diana's mother with a pot of Beef Tea.

****

The remaining dinner parties happened in a volley. The last was the Martha Stewart party. Each guest's wine glass came with a silver charm—a terrier, thimble-sized pair of Jimmy Choo heels, miniature tennis racket. Refilling Diana's glass, E. interrupted a conversation about Monique's recent publication, "Lamp chimneys for hosting a midsummer night's party. Consider a modern Friendsgiving at your renovated farmhouse!"

The following Monday, E. sipped a glass of water and watched for the mail. She straightened the fridge magnet of the Colosseum holding Rick's photo. E. was adept at the rules of a game. At a birthday party in fourth grade, during hide and seek, E. had stayed on her belly in the cold mud hours after other girls quit and flitted in lit windows. The birthday girl's mother phoned her ex-husband, a state trooper, and other parents joined in the search, but E. stayed the longest undiscovered. She could wait for the thank-you cards that never arrived in that day's post, or the next. *Speed ze-ro six knots, ladies. Ready to dive.*

Alexandria Peary

Alexandria Peary is the author of nine books, most recently, *Battle of Silicon Valley at Daybreak* (2021). Her writing has appeared in the *North American Review*, *Yale Review*, and more. She is the Poet Laureate of New Hampshire and specialises in mindful writing.

Birdie

Reaching up, my fingertips feel the sticky on the windowsill. Beccy spilled her squash there last night. I stand on the stool and rub the pale orange blobs with the stiff corner of my pillow. Now, I can climb up and do my looking. The wood feels cold on my feet, so I scrunch my toes and am glad my pull-ups keep my bottom cosy.

Outside, on the grass in the square, a bike with little wheels on the sides has died. If he lets us out to play today, I will check the poking-out bits of the tyres with my tongue and save how it feels for later. Sun is bright on the block of flats over the way. It makes their black and blue graffiti dance.

Graffiti must be fun. Yesterday at nursery, they took us outside in the playground to draw on the pavement. We put our hands into an old ice cream tub full of chalks as fat as Love Heart packets. They fitted just right in my hand, and I curled my fingers around, like when I'm hiding my sweeties. Love Hearts have writing on them inside a heart-shaped ridge. I like to rub the fizzy on my tongue, then crunch the words so they will stay inside me.

On the pavement, I used the orange and yellow chalks most, but I scratched a blue cloud too, and green for grass under the birdie tree, and pink for bunny rabbits, which aren't pink in real life. I know that because I'm not a stupid little fucker like he tells Mummy. I didn't draw the birdie though, because she's my secret. After the rain washed all our pictures away, Susan told us we could draw other ones later.

Susan is the lady who shows us things to do at my nursery. She says I don't need to wear my nappy anymore because I'm a big girl. I'm bigger than Mummy's new baby. I am one, two, three, four.

Leaning back on the windowsill, I lift my unicorn nightie to rub the bobbly front of my pull-ups – it isn't really a nappy, but I haven't told that to Susan because I know to keep my filthy, stupid trap shut. Using the grey curve around the top of my thumbnail, I trace all over the yellow and pink, upside-down picture on my pull-ups. They didn't print the picture the right way up, so I tilt my head to see it better. I think it's a picture of a birdie, like the one that sings outside every morning. That one's not yellow except on its pointy beak.

Every morning, when I hear my birdie, I play Scan with my finding finger. I trace all across the block of flats, and along the grass square. Every time, the birdie is in the tree next to the flats. She is light black with dots on her chest.

I like the birdie's cartoon songs. She makes the same up-and-down-the-stairs-singing from her branch every morning after the man birdie has flied off somewhere to catch a wriggly worm. In the daytime, the man birdie comes back because the little birdie stops singing. Maybe the man birdie shouted *shut up, shut it now, you little fucker.* Or maybe the little birdie just learned to be quiet.

Around my get-to-bed time, the man birdie must go away for a while again because the little birdie sings until the moon gets shiny. I bet Susan knows what *shut up* is in birdie speak. I think if I asked her, she would laugh at me and say I am funny. She does that when Chloe asks her questions, even if they are not funny ones. Chloe goes to my nursery. She asks questions *all* the time.

As I am drawing a sunshine shape in the wet on the window, my tummy rumbles so loud that Beccy looks up. I wait, sure he will shout at me from next door to *shut the fuck up,* but he doesn't. Him and Mummy must be still asleep. I stretch out the front of my pull-ups and poke at my tummy. It will have to bloody well wait until after Mummy and him have smoked enough for wanting morning toast.

Pushing my chin against my chest, I squint. The picture on my pull-ups got blurred while I was asleep. It always goes like that by Saturday, but I can't get a new one until tomorrow. That's okay because I know how to fix it.

At nursery, they have pens that feel slippy when you press your finger against the end. That makes a teeny colour freckle which tastes like vinegar. Yesterday, I took a pink pen and a yellow one and hid them in the hole in my coat pocket because of the weekend. Saturday and Sunday is the weekend. That's when I only have my own, no-colour dry pens to pretend with.

Did you know, the nursery is open every day of the weekdays? Chloe goes there on Monday, Tuesday, Wednesday, Thursday *and* Friday. I know all my days. But I can't go to nursery every day because there is no money tree where we live.

Lots of buses go past the road in front of my nursery. I would like to climb up the big step into one and go on a far travel to find a money tree. That can't happen because Mummy pays money to get on the bus and Mister Driver wouldn't let me pay in Beccy's plastic coins. My hand clamps over my mouth and a giggle breathes into my palm. I would like to find some money that fell out of a grown-up's pocket in a shop. Then, I could give it to Mummy and she could pay the nursery to let me go there on all the Chloe days. I think about this, then punch my thigh. Stupid, stupid. Mummy would tell him if I found money. He would use it to buy stinky baccy and long cans of beer with white plastic holes holding them together.

A car with squeaky brakes stops on the road below. It is blue and clean, like the holes in the clouds. I think this new car will drive away, but it parks. I rub a bigger circle onto the window. A lady gets out wearing a long top to match her blue car. The boot stretches one of her arms up as it opens. There are grey and orange bags inside. She slings a big grey bag over her shoulder, then hooks a mask around her ears to hide her face.

We live on the second floor, and I have better eyes than Mummy, so I can see the blue lady has a red ribbon hanging around her neck with a card dangling off it. She checks her mobile phone, swipes it off, and puts it in her pocket. I watch her walking to the building until my nose squashes against the wet glass and she disappears.

The buzzer in our flat makes a taser noise like from the police programmes he watches. Beccy and me look at each other with pointing-gun eyes. She puts down her pretend baked bean can, then hugs the green teddy she got for letting the doctor put a plaster caster on her arm. I slide down off the windowsill and hide the nursery pens in the hole in my coat.

From their room next door, I hear his deep, waking-up mumbling. He says something to Mummy in the cross voice he uses when she is too tired to play their night-time games. Mummy answers in her dinner-is-burning voice. I think one of them picks the baby up because it makes a sound like a bony kitten.

Again, *buzzzzzz!* That blue lady is brave. I put my hands over my ears, but he doesn't shout. Instead, I hear his slow feet *slap, slap, slap* against the hallway floor, all the way to the intercom. Beccy calls it the *entercon*. She says *laminated* milk, too. Beccy is more littler than me, so it's allowed.

He coughs and does lumpy snorting in the back of his throat. 'Yeah?'

In a lady's voice, I hear one electric word: 'Midwife.'

He doesn't have a wife anymore because he has Mummy instead. A faraway buzz opens the door downstairs. I hear Mummy get up too, slippering into the lounge with the kitten baby.

The front door lock clunks and he uses his shopping voice to ask the lady to come in. They talk in the lounge. Me and Beccy blink at each other. She twists her dummy in her mouth and squeezes her green teddy, then follows me. I try the door. He forgot to lock it last night. We creep along the hallway. He says something and we stop and hold our breaths. When we hear them chatting like the ladies at nursery do, we tiptoe some more. There is no door for the lounge, so we stand just inside the floor line to see.

Mummy is sitting in the armchair. Her dressing gown that looks like a leopard has a patch of baby sick on one shoulder and her hair is all messy. On the sofa, he is wearing jogging bottoms and a smile that makes my tummy feel tight.

The blue lady with the mask turns her head to look at us. I think she knows about the pens I took, which makes me need the toilet, so it is good I am wearing my pull-ups, just in case. I want to swallow but my mouth is too dry. Then, the lady doesn't say about my pens. Instead, her eyes crinkle around the edges like Susan's do when she reads us all a story.

The lady has tucked her card inside her top pocket. The red ribbon is hanging down like a sway of long hair that ladies have on perfume adverts. In only one hand, she is holding Mummy's new baby. It is naked, lying on its front, a wriggle of arms and legs. I know it is a boy. When they came home from hospital on Tuesday, he told Mummy that not another girl is better.

The blue lady doesn't ask about Mummy's old baby or tell Beccy to take her dummy out. In a Susan-from-nursery voice, she says hello to us. Beccy squeezes my hand. We don't look at him or his black sofa. We don't say hello back to the lady. We are not stupid little shits with big mouths.

Twisting her body away from us, the lady lays the new baby on a machine like a plastic cot. That makes the baby cry for a bottle. He doesn't shout at the baby or shout at us to *get out now* or point his fat grey finger at the doorway, but we can tell from his stillness that he is thinking it. The blue lady hasn't turned around to ask us our names or how old we are yet. New grown-ups always ask that. Like police. We reverse over the line and gallop up the hallway to our room.

I climb back on my windowsill. Beccy and her teddy buy the little plastic can of baked beans from the corner shop on our mattress. This time, she makes her and Teddy dinner using yesterday's morning toast plate. Mummy bought me that plate in the Barnardo shop because I liked the picture of Winnie the Pooh. That picture is all rubbed off now. All that's left is two red splotches like Mummy used to get on her cheeks when he shouted.

Outside, in the sun's shadow, the graffiti has stopped dancing and Birdie has stopped singing.

***

Tracey Montague

Tracey Montague is an (as yet) unpublished novelist and prize-winning poet and a contributor to the *Writers' & Artists'* blog. She has taught philosophy and world music and has also been a university press editor. Currently, she is a midwife to babies as well as words.

Certificate of Infertility

I wasn't bothered that an unsmiling trainee doctor signed my certificate of infertility, although qualified doctors would show some white teeth before breaking bad news. I didn't care that I'd joined the club of men whose pumps couldn't inflate wombs. The worry about my lineage becoming extinct didn't even occur to me.

What upsets me now, months later, is that my wife is pregnant, and I don't know who's responsible – a guy, a god, or a ghost. The truth remains that lies have always been the honey and sugar of our marriage. Even before we married, I told her that a Range Rover Jeep was mine, and she cried when I returned the car to the owner after our wedding. She told me she was a fresh petal and no horny bee had perched on her, but I later met an Olympic auditorium under her skirt. Since then, I've refused to reveal to her that during the Boko Haram war a bullet speared my groin, damaging my reproductive tubes. That's why I don't shave my groin, so as to hide the scar.

Now she wants to convince me that I'm the new blood in her womb, that my fruit is functional with seeds. She smiles and rubs her hand on her bulging stomach. Women can be funny. Very, very funny.

She points at her stomach. 'Darling, this baby is going to look exactly like you,' she says, sitting on the couch.

I frown. 'How do you know?'

'You were at your best the day you ejaculated into me.'

I shake my head. What else can a retired soldier do? If a woman doesn't kill a man, nothing else can kill him.

But I'm going to unearth the source of this pregnancy today by consulting a famous witchdoctor, Baba Jesus-Mohammed, who a friend has strongly recommended. I don't have the huge money for a DNA test. And, anyway, witchdoctors have been saving our lives for ages, revealing secrets through their spiritual diagnoses, long before white men violated us with digital machines, and asked us to abandon our gods.

I'm about to leave my house to board an eight-hour bus to the village, and I have to lie again to my wife.

'Sweetie, I'm going for an official duty,' I say, my mind on my ominous suitcase hidden in a coppice of hibiscuses outside our gate.

'Go well,' she says, smiling. 'When you return, we'll agree on a name for your lookalike in my womb.'

The suitcase is full of sacrificial items: a white fowl, cowries, red candles, white sand, red cloths, a small earthenware pot, a tortoise, and duck feathers. She mustn't see these things; God, she mustn't because as far as she knows I'm a good

Christian who shouldn't be caught with pagan objects.

I snort and leave.

The moving yellow bus is full of stern-looking people, men and women whose problems are engraved on their faces. From their serious looks I can tell we're all going to see the same witchdoctor. We Nigerians are restless souls. We combine charms and Jesus Christ in order to achieve anything, and we attribute the power to only Jesus Christ. Our own Jesus Christ has been credited with many unmerited accomplishments.

Our bus coughs, jerks, and picks up speed again.

I tap a man sitting to my left. Both of us are in the front seat. 'Are you sure the witchdoctor isn't a river that dries up when needed most?' I ask.

'No,' he says. 'For every problem, he knows a god that solves it.'

'And we have to pay our dues to the gods?'

'Exactly.'

'Is it right for Christians to partake in idol worship?'

He chuckles. 'Man, there's no right or wrong in this matter-o,' he says. 'Even Muslims don't trust Allah and Prophet Mohammed these days. They must visit African witchdoctors to verify things. Students patronise them, too, to make their exams easy. They hope the witchdoctors can reveal the exam questions in advance.'

'Oh, really?'

'Of course, the witchdoctors can even become invisible, sneak into the hall, and write exams for the students.'

'This is my first time going to see Baba Jesus-Mohammed,' I say.

'You won't be disappointed, trust me.'

Now we've spent seven hours and forty-five minutes on the road, but we're still going, hoping, going, almost there.

Finally, we arrive and walk to the reception desk in single file. The witchdoctor has his shrine inside a three-storey building. It seems he alone lives in this silent neighbourhood. A lady in a crumpled skirt gives each of us a number. Thank God, I'm number one.

She details the rules and regulations, 'Remove your footwear. Cut your fingernails. Items of jewellery aren't allowed inside.' She hiccups. 'Women should remove their underwear. They must be naked before the witchdoctor. I'm afraid that any woman having her period can't enter. Menstruation renders the witchdoctor powerless and blind. Any man or woman who's had sex the previous night, I'm sorry, can't see Baba Jesus-Mohammed.' She coughs. 'At the door, before you enter, you must shout your name seven times. On the stool near the door, there's a razor blade. Pick it up, cut your middle finger open, and dab the blood on the door to mark your presence.'

She hiccups again and swallows her spittle.

'Is that all, sister?' I ask.

'No, sir,' she says. 'You must submit your photo to Baba Jesus-Mohammed. Is that clear?'

'Yes, yes,' we say, nodding and glancing at one another.

None of us dares to question the rules.

It's my turn, and I perform all the drama at the door before climbing the flight of stairs. When I get into the shrine, I find Baba Jesus-Mohammed seated on the bare floor. He flashes me a spooky smile. I also feel his warm welcome through his eyes the colour of carrot juice. The Bible and the Qur'an are opened in front of him, with a statuette of a local deity which squats and stares at him. A blazing red candle stands between the holy books. There's a framed drawing of Arabic lettering on the wall, hanging alongside a big cross with moons and stars carved into the four edges. The cross carries a decaying, full-size crocodile nailed to its centre. The protruding nail looks rusty. The place smells like a loaded mortuary without electricity, and, at times, the stench of rotten fish makes its way into my nostrils. I pinch my nose. Above us, a red bulb glows, colouring a white pillow and a thick mattress in one corner. By the mattress is a pack of condoms. A black goat eats fresh grass near a bony, sad dog slurping water from the remains of a broken plastic bucket. Greasy clothes are hung on the clothesline connecting two opposite walls with peeling white paint. There's a dictionary and a calculator on a short stool near the grass-eating goat. I wonder if the animal is a journalist or a mathematician.

Baba Jesus-Mohammed wears a white gown, and faces the holy books. His head is covered with a red turban. He holds a big padlock in his left hand. The padlock could be the most potent object in the room – for locking the devil.

He asks me to offload my sacrificial items in a corner and sit before him. My tortoise crawls out, and my fowl squawks. I'm happy the animals are still alive.

'Where's your photo?'

'Here,' I say, sitting down and handing it over.

He throws it into a basket.

Baba starts chanting, 'In the name of Allah, I pray through Jesus Christ, our Lord in Heaven. Hallowed be the name of Sango, the able god of thunder and fire. I beseech the kingdom of Ogun, the iron god of ages, to come down now. Thy will be done on earth through the special powers of Ifa, the god that owns my divination.'

I notice he has one incisor missing and a gold tooth replacing another.

He holds out a needle and asks me to lean forward. Jittery blood hurries through my veins. My breathing and heartbeat quicken. I exhale loudly. He pierces my forehead, and I feel the sharp pain as blood gushes out. He asks me not to touch it. I hit my chest to show bravery. He picks up a glass cup and asks me to allow the blood to drip into it. When he's collected enough, he snaps open a bottle of schnapps and pours alcohol into the glass cup, half full. He spits into it, mixes everything with his middle finger, and holds the cup towards me.

'Drink it,' he says.

I recoil, eyeing my suitcase and the exit. 'What?'

'Drink.'

I collect the cup and sip once, grimacing as I swallow. And then I gulp down everything.

He nods, collecting the cup. 'What can I do for you?'

'I'd like to know who got my wife pregnant.'

He falls silent, shuts his eyes, and opens them again.

'Oh, it's very clear,' he says. 'Your wife isn't pregnant.'

'What?' I burst out. 'Baba, are you sure of what you're saying?'

'Jesus Christ! Don't doubt the gods. They see farther than we do.'

Has my wife lied to me again, perhaps strapping a football under her gown? She shouldn't lie about something as serious as pregnancy. Is she sick in the stomach? My mind tries to convince me this man must have impregnated her and he's here to confuse me, but I dismiss the thought.

'But, Baba—'

He holds out his hand. 'Have you paid?'

'No, Baba.'

'Allah, in that case, there's been a terrible mistake. I thought you paid the receptionist. I can't see clearly until you pay. I divine better when my stomach is full. Please drop five thousand naira into that bowl.'

He points.

I dip my hand into my pocket and pull out the money. 'Here it is, Baba,' I say, throwing it into the bowl.

He picks up the money and buries it deep in the bag sitting beside him. He sighs, then shuts his eyes, and opens them again. 'Let me ask once more. What do you want to find out?'

'Am I the one who's sent my wife on a nine-month journey?'

'Let me check.' He turns the pages of the Bible and mutters Arabic words while leafing through the Qur'an. 'Oh, the gods are having their siesta. They can't talk to me right now.' He grabs a bronze bell and rings it seven times. 'I want to wake them up, but they're all snoring.'

'Baba, that's not what I've come here to learn.'

'What do you want?'

'The truth about my wife.'

'You say she's pregnant?'

'Yes, Baba.'

'How often do you have sex with her?'

'As often as I want.'

'You must have impregnated her, *wallahi.*'

'But a doctor has said I'm sterile.'

'What?'

I spot my wife's photo among the sea of other photos stuck to the walls and cringe.

'Baba, that's my wife's photo,' I say, pointing. 'She's been here!'

'Shut up and listen to me. Man, you talk too much. Leave your wife alone and focus on your own problem. Afternoon is a wrong period to visit me because the gods can't reveal the truth at this hour of sleep. You can come back another day with more money. I recommend the morning hours. That's when the gods are getting out of bed with no sleep in their eyes. Please, go!'

The goat bleats, its voice furious. The miserable dog growls, and I know my time is up. I weep, struggling to hold back tears, as I step into the landing and run downstairs. When I get home, I'll weigh my tongue and mind, and determine what next to do.

Previously Published in UEA MA Anthologies 2019 (Prose Fiction) by Egg Box Publishing.

Jekwu Anyaegbuna

Jekwu won the Commonwealth Short Story Prize for Africa, a fiction fellow at the *Elizabeth Kostova Foundation for Creative Writing* in Bulgaria. His fiction has been in *Granta, The White Review,* and *Transition.* He won the 2023 *Poetry London Prize.*

In the Face Of(f)

The male plug has entered far enough back into the TV's female connector to take. But what reappears is our governor (The Goon we call him), partly in pixels and still expounding on the state of emergency. His transmission erased the dead monitor's Barbie doll-size reflection of Jane standing behind me near the maroon couch, clasping the green throw she'd just sat covered in. A frozen calm. I want her to appreciate that I'm taking some kind of action, although I can't see what I'm doing, fumble-pinching the cable on the backside of the television, my cheek splayed against The Goon's. Balancing on my knees like a rocking chair about to keel over, with my other hand, my left, I simultaneously steady the plasma TV and keep my second-trimester bump—our first baby—from hitting the console's corner.

"See!" Jane says. "You didn't change anything."

I twist to face the 32" frame. The governor wets his lips.

"No. Not yet," I say, and consider unscrewing the nut for the second time. Why not? It seems a fitting thing to do.

The Goon had interrupted the regular programming's documentary True North Going South to declare a state of emergency because of Richard, the category 5 Hurricane that passed south of us three days ago. "The dikes didn't hold," The Goon spat. "And The Army Corps of Engineers, whom we'd trusted, will have to answer for that."

Of his scalp's runway streak of baldness (on screen, it was sunburned), Jane often says, "a thought might land," and I'll twang something like, "Penetration is another matter," or "And never take off again." Between ourselves, we can only address politics jokingly. Including: How many people does it take to screw in a light bulb in 2080? None.

"We've always had bad weather. It's a matter of preparing for it." The governor's crown reddened like the hot zones on the globe that Jane and I had just watched.

The documentary's 14-second timeline—starting in 1880 when temperature recording began worldwide—had shown Earth like the proverbial candle burning at both ends. As the simulation concluded, the North and South Poles both glowed reddish purple. And Jane, with whom I volunteer on a farm to learn how to run our own ranch (I dream because I know how), and whom I plan to have four in-vitro kids with (each of us carrying two), sat ash-pale next to me in the sofa, puffing worse than at Lamaze practice, as if she was running out of oxygen, (it happens more and more frequently). We've never talked about why. Nor have we discussed what crops to grow—which implies the hope we will later. It does.

"Unbelievable," Jane gasped at the TV.
"I know," I said. "I know."

This was when The Goon's broadcast had first appeared.
"The problem," he sputtered, "is in all the radicals' heads."
So I got up, went over to the TV, and banged the skinny top the same way my grandma had done whenever her tube set went snowy. And I suddenly felt old, like Oma, who bore seven children, lived to be ninety-eight, and, for years, asserted that her daily "nips" of whiskey eventually would build up enough residual alcohol in her system to self-ignite. Eco-cremation, she called it. "I don't want to take up any more space."
I pounded harder on the TV.
"That's so not helping," Jane said. Her breathing rhythmic yet fast.

(The Goon had cut in as the narrator, Liam Neeson, explained that a person's breathing added 0.8 kilograms of CO_2 into the atmosphere a day, which for the 9-plus billion population amounted to around 3 gigatons of CO_2 a year. (But who is counting?)

As I rubbed my pregnant belly and held my breath (gestures that felt like actions), I wondered what the CO_2 numbers were before man walked the Earth. And to keep the world at bay, I could have shut off the television. Instead, needing to do something, something physical, that's when I started decoupling the cable feed the first time.
I did hear the dull thud of cushions behind me but didn't want it to mean Jane had gotten up, as her small upright version in the blank display affirmed, and I took my time (wishing it could be indefinite) inspecting the cable's conductor for corrosion before reconnecting it. With the glass again cool against my skin, my angled profile cast a charcoal silhouette on the TV's empty display, next to doll-sized Jane, still standing.
I fantasized that once I'd recoupled the cable, the public service announcement could be over, and the documentary back and on to the part where Neeson would offer solutions. (I'm not delusional, I merely don't know for what change or chance to hope. But I hope there's still time.)

The lock nut's crisscrossed metal cut into my clammy fingers. I squeeze and twist. It's beginning to hurt.
And then the monitor refills with the pixilated governor.
"He's someone's son," Jane mumbles.
"I know," I say.

"A state of emergency is the only way to proceed." His mouth wide open, his slimy uvula and swollen tonsils pulsating near my nose.

I align my legs underneath my belly to push off and away, but my sweaty left hand braced on top of the TV slips. The moment feels suspended. I grab for the edge of the console and miss.

In a last-ditch effort, I twist my torso and ram my head into The Goon. The screen shatters. There: I've changed the picture. Blood trickles down my forehead (it'll stop). Behind me, Jane weeps. I want it to be of gratitude but know better: the tears will become a river, then a flood.

Pernille AEgidius Dake

Born and raised in Denmark, Pernille AEgidius Dake winter bathes in the Baltic and knits afghans without dropped stitches. Her work appeared in *Adelaide Literary Magazine*, *ArLiJo*, *Beyond Words*, *Burningword Literary Journal*, *Write Launch* and elsewhere.

Covenants, Considered

When he called you beautiful it was wrong but you let him do it anyway, word meaning more than it should to your body bearing the weight of youth's memory, furious feet kicking their way out of your womb. Once taut belly; soft, striated. Your husband, whose fruits shaped your belly's loaves, can look at his progeny, feel satisfied. You: utility, a vessel, whether anyone wants to admit it. Me-changes don't bother him. You should be grateful; he understands biology of aging cells.

Words he used to whisper – sabrosura, mi cielo – haven't left his lips in years. You want to hear them, are too proud to ask. *Deliciousness. My heaven.* It translates as *my sky;* you like that better. To be blue and wide, to carry the weight of thunderstorms. Sought by birds, traced by falling stars; really this is all you want.

Hon and *babe* carry no poetry; perhaps their endless repetition in the sea of wipes, cleats, footballs, lunchboxes is why you never became a poet.

You want to believe poetry exists in the cheap hotel room off the highway where no one knows you, a long drive from your son's preschool, where he chews on crayons, takes off his shoes, buries his legs into damp sand. The thought of his bare feet, his teacher's pale hands against his chubby flesh cramming his toes back into socks, makes you turn around.

*****

You drive to the hotel, leave. The man waiting speaks Spanish, like your husband, but his accent is more pronounced. Finally he says *beautiful* again, in English, Spanish, something in between, language disregarding resistance. You make it to the parking lot and lock your car, ignoring scattered cheerios, empty juice boxes, hoping he won't walk you to your car after. The whole time you wonder what you're seeking from men who speak a language you don't understand, why one man's journey across the boundaries of tongue and border isn't enough, why you are seeking another.

Or being sought. To be fair you sought nothing.

You're afraid, but not too afraid. Maybe just as afraid as you should be. Many things can make a body tremble.

You seek poetry. This man's hands are pen, prompt, lyre of eons. Whatever love song thrums in his fingers soothes the traces of your silvered jumbles of cells, which never recovered from bouts of hyperemesis, how your seams were restitched into something that will never again be whole. Isn't that what it means to be a mother?

Maybe the poem hides in the nest of another's woman's hair, dark strands fallen between headboards, strands weary maids won't see. You notice because your inner poet has come alive in new arms of new man whose taste is wild, like fire, mean like liquor at the bottom of the bottle. It makes you sick but still you just want to drink until all the things that make you hate yourself, including this very moment, are burned away.

*****

This man's attention thrums so different from the quietly efficient way your husband fucks you, in the room filled with pull-ups, trucks, Legos pressing their shape into your foot. Another women's hair fallen into slimspace between headboards sings a song wildly different from song of six-year-old-son, with lost socks, dream-demons, pushing himself between you and your husband, so even if your husband wanted to fuck you in that *sabrosura* way it could never happen.

Next time, the room is clean. You don't need poetry of hair; poetry of his fingers enough for you to find his need in your rhythm and know for sure that even old liquor burns, that even burning, sometimes, isn't enough.

You might have gone on fucking him forever but he, with his poetry, Old-World-romance-fingers wanting to touch every inch of you, insisted on washing your hair, so very English-patient of him. He found the thing on your head, dark, tiny seed-sprout of toxins.

Another rage-red round of humiliation at your body. His reassurances terrify you, so you delete him from your contacts, quietly get tested for STDs. After all, cancer is for husbands.

You survive. Your marriage survives, even when you burn with knowing your husband never would have found that smirking growth. Your child stops chewing crayons. You know he'll be a smoker anyway. You stopped smoking when pregnant but sometimes, still, miss the taste of fire in your mouth.

When you think about your betrayal, you remember
spiced-sweet tongue ---
sharp smell of fire –

another
woman's
hair.

Kathleen Furin

Kathleen Furin earned her MFA from New York University. She is the recipient of the Eludia Award for her collection *Last Sunrise*, forthcoming from Sowilo Press. Her work features in American Literary Review, Evanescent, Permafrost Magazine, amongst others.

Does the wind blow colder at home?

(For Noel)

'You can sit here.'

Darcy scooped up his bag, his iPhone, and a bag of lollies. His ribs hurt a little, but not so much he needed to grimace.

'Are you sure?' The woman smiled. Her son clambered over the departure room seats under the stern eye of his father. 'You're a gentleman.'

Darcy moved to the sill beneath the large airport windows. As he rearranged his things, a notification lit up on his phone. CALL MUM – TELL HER! In the thirty-five minutes between handing in his high school dorm keys and arriving at the airport, he'd been transfixed by the fluttering ribbons on the Uber's AC vents. With fifteen minutes to boarding, now would be as good a time as any.

He popped a Fantale in his mouth and read the wrapper, *Roy Halston Frowick 1932-1990*. The boy stopped running and watched Darcy put down his lolly bag.

'You want one?' Darcy started to ask.

'Get here, Jackson. Sit down.' The dad pulled his son onto a seat. His leathery fingers engulfed the boy's shoulder. Beneath heavy eyebrows, the man glared at Darcy, looking him over as if searching for clues. *The Mr Nelson once-over*, Darcy called it. His eponymous hometown primary school teacher had lacked subtlety when treating his students fairly. His favourites could attend the canteen early for lunch orders or run errands out of class. Darcy's ilk received a suspicious eye, one giving him an excuse to ask for the bins to be emptied.

Darcy rubbed his chest. Perhaps his ribs hurt more than he realised.

Five minutes before boarding, Darcy took a deep breath and dialled. The silences between each ringtone stretched into aeons, and the chime repeated enough times for Darcy to consider hanging up.

'Please don't be Dad,' he whispered.

'Hello?' The voice of his mother – all colourful wine gums and saliva-dampened tissues to wipe your face – sounded in the earpiece. 'Darcy?'

'Hi, Mum. How are you?'

She sighed. Darcy could not tell whether the heat of a northern town inspired her exasperation or if she knew what he was up to. He tried again.

'What have you been doing today?'

'Oh, I'm still struggling with my seedlings.' As his mother related her trouble with nurturing wildflowers, Darcy heard his dad cough in the background.

Stories of the Pheladenia Deformis continued. 'That's the blue orchid, Darcy.'

The coarse barking from a living room five hundred kilometres away drew his attention. The familiar vocal tones were all there like dismantled insults shouted through a bedroom door. Each burst of air from his dad's lungs sounded like a reflection of disappointment, a moral jab potentially escalating into a rage sparked by his son's shortcomings.

'Do you think the wind blows colder at home?' She asked in the way a magician might say *is this your card?* And with the same effect.

'Pardon?'

'At night, when it blows in off the sea. That's why these seeds just won't grow.'

'That must be it, Mum.' Darcy swallowed. 'Maybe give them more shelter.'

'Will you be home for your things?' He knew the sum of his childhood possessions, two Lego sets and an unused cricket bat, were keystones for his mother. Since he'd left for high school, Darcy repeatedly told his mother to toss them out. The topic was part of their conversational routine. After six years, Darcy knew she enjoyed keeping his room as he'd left it.

'No, you keep them. I have everything with me.' He looked at his small carry-on and thought of the school uniform, its scuffed elbows and bloodied collar, hanging in his dorm room. He couldn't have abandoned the outfit any faster.

That morning, Darcy pulled on the t-shirt from his year twelve play in a fit of liberty. He'd waited months to wear it, and, in hindsight, he might have waited to change in the Uber. Keen to hand out their last licks, a chuckling posse of graduating boarders used his attire as an excuse to bid him farewell. Still, no blood on his favourite top was a silver lining.

'I'm flying straight to Sydney. I'm not coming home.' Darcy put his hand over his mouth.

'Oh, I miss your face.' Her voice trembled. 'Such a young man, now. Seventeen years old.'

'I would have loved to see you too, Mum.'

'I wish things could've been easier for you.' *She sees a strident wildflower, not the verdant carnation.*

'The academy said yes, remember?'

'Do you...' she hesitated, 'want to speak with your –'

'I think we're boarding, Mum.'

They exchanged farewells, promising to talk soon. Darcy hung up his phone. He slumped against the cold glass and glanced at the flight board. Boarding *soon*, anyway.

From the window, Darcy looked across the airport tarmac to the scrubland and the hills beyond. Every feature of the landscape held uncomfortable memories: sports carnivals, school excursions, a walk from the dorms to the deli, only to turn back at the last moment when he saw other boarders vaping by the store's bins. Deep within this thorny domain lived his mother. He dared to think if she could have made his life easier. He wondered who abandoned whom?

Boarding calls for his flight were announced. He sighed and condensation misted upon the window. To his left, a queue to enter the plane. To Darcy's right, a clinical-looking exit past expensive coffees and magazine racks. He fell in behind the family from before. The boy, beside himself with glee, couldn't wait to get on the flight.

The passengers filed down the tunnel. Some rummaged through their belongings, already searching for a lost boarding pass or a missing phone app. Others looked ahead with the confidence of experienced travellers. In front of Darcy, the mother he'd spoken to earlier reached down and took her boy's hand.

'Fuck,' Darcy muttered, desperately wanting to turn around. Yet, caught up in the herd and unwilling to inconvenience anyone by stopping, he lumbered forward to the plane.

'Oh, there's an issue with this seat,' said the flight attendant. 'Would you be able to wait here while I get everyone else aboard?'

Darcy stood to one side and tried to be skinny against the bulkhead as the rest of the passengers brushed past him. He smiled and apologised when people thumped him with their bags. From his dim corner, the sky bridge glowed white. In that bright tube, spacious and luminous, the air looked easy to breathe.

'This way, Sir,' the attendant indicated to Darcy to follow her down the aisle. 'We have personnel returning to Sydney but not working on this flight. You booked an emergency exit row seat, but those have been allocated to staff.'

The seated passengers, already impatient for take-off, glared at Darcy as he passed. Like a murderer following the bailiff through a crowded courtroom, the young man did his best to avoid eye contact.

'Here you are.'

Darcy looked up to see the family from the departure lounge. At the far end, the mother sat next to her boy. Then a spare seat, covered by the dad's book and headphones, and next, the disgruntled man himself, clearly unhappy at the prospect of losing the extra room.

'Sir, perhaps you could move next to your son and allow this gentleman to sit on the aisle.'

The man exhaled through pursed lips as he fumbled with his lap-sash buckle.

'Thank you,' the attendant repeated as the hulk of a man, now three times his former size within the confines of the cabin, moved over one seat. 'We'll be taxiing out shortly.'

Darcy slid into the aisle seat, avoiding contact with the dad's thigh-like forearms hanging over the armrest. He read the wrapper of another sweet, *Tennessee Williams 1911-1983*, but couldn't bear to eat it. The cabin's air thickened, mixing with the atmosphere of impatience among the passengers. Above, a no-smoking sign blinked on and off as if it, too, couldn't decide whether to commit to this flight.

Darcy looked across the window seats and out onto the tarmac. *What if I never returned?* He took out his phone, intending to activate airplane mode and saw the wallpaper. A photograph of his mother, enthusiastically hugging him at the year ten dinner, smiled back. Quickly, he typed.

'Perhaps you could come over this Christmas or after I'm settled in? '

The man sitting next to him stood as Darcy waited for a reply.

'Do you think Dad would leave the farm to travel?????' his Mum texted back.

The farm. Of course, the farm. Being busy with the business accounted for his father's absence from school performances and ensured Darcy needed to stay at the dorm during holidays. Adding an extra body at home would only detract from meaningful farm work. Darcy turned on airplane mode and absently began flicking through photos.

Four generations old, the phone held only a dozen pictures. There were two from the year ten dinner, one of Stout, the family's blue heeler, and another of his Lego sets – before Dad broke them apart. He lingered on a selfie taken on the six-hour coach trip between the farm and Perth back in year seven. Not for the first time, he thought, *when you're hoping for a sorry – but all you get is it's best you move away.*

Darcy looked at his younger, bruised face. *How much pain did that boy have ahead of him?* At the time, he'd thought Boarding School would be a reprieve. *Am I running away now? How much pain do I have ahead of me?* He swiped the picture away and paused.

The last picture, one his drama teacher had sent him, showed him standing on the school stage at the finale of Oliver the Musical. Blue lights beamed down around him. Silhouettes of cheering parents framed the bottom of the shot. He stood above them all. Arms raised high, a smile as bright as the stage lights beamed back at the adoring crowd. The teachers all said he would steal the show. Ms Johns cried when she met him backstage.

'Your parents must be so proud,' the mother said. She'd swapped seats with her husband and looked over Darcy's shoulder at his photo.

'Yes.' He knew it sounded like a lie. 'Mum is.'

The woman looked back to her son as he tapped on an iPad.

'You don't always find your answers at home,' she said.

Darcy turned off airplane mode as he walked out of Sydney Domestic. He waited for the phone's messages to update while rummaging for the last Fantale, *Harvey Bernard Milk 1930-1978*. Gradually, his phone returned to life; the time zone changed, the weather updated, and a message appeared on the screen.

'You know, I fancy flying over by myself.' Darcy felt a tear drop from his nose as he double-checked his mother as the sender. 'Xmas in Sydney – I could check out the academy?'

'Hey, I like your T-shirt!'

'Pardon?' Darcy looked up, searching for the owner of the sweet voice.

The stranger kept walking but looked back and threw a thumbs-up sign, 'Love the shirt, man.'

By the time Darcy said thank you, the stranger had rounded a corner and disappeared. Darcy ran the palm of his hand across his t-shirt. His bruised ribs itched but no longer ached.

David Wildsmith

David Wildsmith is an award-winning writer and presenter. He writes novels, short stories, film scripts and plays. Drawing on his own experiences, his work expresses abandonment and displacement as faced by expatriates. He produces the Strange Reads YouTube channel.

Doreen's Last Day

Doreen had decided to die.

Rewind to this morning.

He had left with his shirt spectacularly un-ironed and a parting shot from the garden pathway. The neighbours had pretended not to notice, but really it had been pretty hard for them not to. Doreen sincerely hoped she wouldn't run into them on the way out. Even the cat seemed to understand that what she needed was emptiness and had helpfully shown her its haughty rear on the way out the cat flap. Mind you, that was only after it had hocked up a large furball on the new cream carpet in the hallway. Just in front of the cat flap.

Oh well. Everything was neat now. The dishwasher was clean, leaky pipe behind it switched off and the routine wet patch on the kitchen floor mopped up. The bed was made and the laundry folded and put away (wardrobe hanging in pleasing colour-graduated order). It was just that empty cotton-bud container still sitting on top of the bathroom cabinet which Doreen had lost the impetus to deal with. Maybe it was a small, final act of rebellion.

Of course it made no difference to her now. These were to be her last hours. She saw the words written in her head like a bad novel. 'The Last Hours of Doreen Price.' Or maybe, 'Doreen Price's Last Dastardly Day'. That had a nice alliterative smack to it in spite of the slight leaning toward melodrama. She said it to herself a few times out loud.

Tidying done, she placed her handbag on the floor next to the bed and her wedding band and phone on the bedside table and left.

Except that had been a false start, because what if she decided not to do it after all? And anyway she needed some cash to pay for posting a letter on the way. (Something to do with work, not a suicide note. She'd decided against one and settled for: 'Just wanted to say to all my friends and family that I love and appreciate them xox' as her Facebook status.)

Right. Take two.

She popped her phone into the pocket of her coat next to the little bottle of bright yellow pills which she had been accruing for the occasion and marched down the high street.

In the post office, the man behind the counter gazed suspiciously at the ten pound note Doreen handed over, flicked it a couple of times and held it up to the light to check it before handing her the change. Four pounds and twenty-four pence. Enough for one last nice coffee. She would pop into the Swan.

Seated in a sunny patch with a well-made latte, the idea of taking the pills began to seem less attractive. Cruelly, the radio started playing 'Dire Straits'. That had always been their music. In the early years when it had all seemed too hard then, she'd listened to it on repeat, soaking her aching soul in the sounds of Knopfler's weeping guitar. As she would be doing now, if she could find her soul.

She decided to take a quick peek at her phone. Switching it on, she found that four people had 'liked' her status (one of whom she couldn't be sure she'd recognise if she tripped over her lying in the street) and *he* had sent her a text message. And a missed call. She didn't open them though. Instead, she pressed the power button tightly until the screen faded to a comforting black over the photo of him smiling in an Italian cafe.

There were hundreds of good things that she could remember about him, possibly thousands, but he'd threatened to leave so she chose not to.

Doreen reached for her coffee cup to find only a sad brown ring of dark grounds at the bottom and a bright red lipstick stain on the rim – which was particularly discouraging as she herself had applied a subtle apricot tone this morning.

She let thoughts trip randomly across her mind. Lucky for her children that she had never got round to having them, she mused. Although whether their good fortune lay in not being about to lose her or in never having had her in the first place, she was undecided about.

One of the patients at her psychiatry practice who continuously harped on about what she euphemistically referred to as 'moving along' seemed, on the other hand, to blame her own children for her depressive state. Doreen had never met the children, but having spent many hours in the company of the mother felt inclined to sympathise with the offspring. Obviously, she didn't mention this. Instead she erm-d a bit, uh-huh-ed politely, wrote meaningless notes (and sometimes her shopping list) in suitably illegible handwriting and sent large, very legible bills for her pains. That woman should either get on with the next world or shut up and save herself a small fortune in this one.

Actually, maybe that was something she herself should have a better idea of before proceeding with the day's plans? Where was the next world? Doreen's head filled with a gush of half-remembered Sunday school lessons and pious confusion. How to unravel that tangled ball of metaphysical wool?!

She was interrupted by the arrival of another cup of coffee and a large slightly sweating man who eased himself, uninvited, into the space opposite her.

'I hope you don't mind,' he leered at her, 'I took the liberty of ordering.' He winked and smoothed his hair with a level of panache approaching deadly.

Doreen touched her face with her left hand, hoping the sight of a wedding band would suffice, until she recalled the rings lying unhelpfully on her bedside table. Could this day get any more unbearable?

Tony noted the small indentation on her ring finger as the woman fiddled with her hair (flirtatious!) and shivered with anticipation. Doreen was clearly his favourite kind of woman – the desperate kind.

Doreen was indeed feeling desperate – just not in the way Tony hoped. She patted her pocket with the little vial of brightly coloured pills and headed for the Ladies.

The click of the tiny bolt as it locked her in seemed unaccountably loud in the small space and she sank down onto the toilet seat. With a curiously anti-climatic lack of fanfare, the moment had come.

The pills were smooth and round and a cheery sunshine yellow. They tasted very sweet as she swallowed them, reminding her of something – she couldn't quite put her finger on what.

Fourteen. Fifteen. Sixteen. Doreen dropped the container into the bin, placed her hands neatly on her knees, closed her eyes and waited.

Nothing.

She opened one eye as someone tried the door handle, then closed it again, scanning her body for unusual sensation. Still nothing.

A creeping anxiety was starting at the base of her spine. What if this was going to be a terribly slow and horrible end? Her alone in this stinking toilet for hours and hours in an agonising approach to her requiem? What if there was a next life after all and she wasn't prepared for it? What if she had made a terrible error in calculation – not merely in how many pills she needed but in taking them at all?

In a reverse process of the grating little life-affirming gratitude exercise she recommended to her patients, Doreen took a deep breath and began to make a list of things that made her cross. Ingrown hairs. Excess facial hair. The things she could've done with her life if she had all the eyebrow-plucking hours back! She could've learned French for example. A sudden deep desire to learn French and an awful sadness at its impossibility began to seep in.

'I want to learn French!' she found herself squeaking, fumbling with the toilet door lock and crashing through the restaurant.

Her phone lay winking with an unread message on the table next to the slimy-looking man. Hadn't she left her phone switched off? Whatever. Her fingers shook as she dialled.

He answered on the second ring. 'Doreen?'

'I don't want to die! I want to learn French!' The impending sobs constricted her airways and she could feel her breathing becoming shallower. Oh heavens! It was starting. 'Please God! If you're there – I don't want to die!'

Simon answered. 'Darling, where are you? What have you done?'

'I'm in The Swan, Simon. Please Simon. Call an ambulance... No, actually, don't hang up!' Doreen paused, pointed at Tony and commanded, 'You! Call an ambulance!'

Simon's voice was repeating something. She struggled to focus on the words. 'Darling! Did you take the yellow pills? The ones in the little glass bottle under the A to Z in your bedside drawer?'

How did he know about those?

'Doreen?'

'Yes. Yes, I did.'

What was he on about?

'A confession? No Simon! I don't care! I can't deal with your confession now! I am dying!'

She didn't sound like a dying woman, Doreen had to admit and wondered at it.

Surely, she should be more regretful and zen. Or deep and tragic and wanting to tell her husband that, in spite of being an absolute pain in the you-know-what, she did actually love him and would miss his very silly sense of humour. And the tea he brought first thing in the morning. Although…

'For goodness sake, Doreen! Listen to me for once!' Hmm. Nope. She definitely wasn't having any of the sentimental thoughts she should by rights have been having.

'If you took the yellow pills you're not dying! At worst you're having a sugar rush.'

A sugar rush?

'Now, sit down, drink a glass of water and try to breathe. I'm on my way to you.'

'Sit down? A sugar rush? Simon! What the hell are you talking about?' At the same time, a sneaky realisation was beginning in the fuzz of Doreen's consciousness. Skittles. Those pills had tasted remarkably like Skittles.

'They're Skittles, Doreen. I've been switching them for Skittles.'

Doreen sat down on the nearest chair and covered her eyes with her free hand, tasting the sugar at the back of her mouth.

She could hear Simon panting now.

'Why, Simon? Why are they Skittles?'

'I was worried. I knew you were... Well I didn't want you to leave me. You know...forever. I mean I didn't want you to leave me at all but I especially…'

'But you said you were leaving?'

A terrible, terrible silence of seconds that lasted like aeons. And then. In a voice more small boy than man, the unthinkable...

'I'm sorry.' An audible swallow. 'I'm sorry.'

A small breathing space was opening in the heavy atmosphere. A gust that felt like... What was that? Hope? She hadn't felt that breeze for some time. 'What was that you said Simon?'

The hard breathing on the other end of the phone had stopped. The phone was dead.

But, there was Simon suddenly bundling into the doorway in disarray, greying hair wild and tears spilling unattractively down his own cheeks. Doreen couldn't remember ever seeing him cry before.

He slumped into the chair next to her. They looked at each other. Matching tears. Unsure where to start.

The waitress glanced at the sweaty middle-aged man and the obviously crazy woman and rolled her eyes. 'More coffee?' Chewing gum pop. Both heads nodded.

Certainly it was going to be an uphill trudge. Undoubtedly it would hurt. Probably there would be a few (or many) more tears and wilful untidiness again at some point (or points) but she would 'not go gentle into that good night'! Not because of Simon per se, nor in spite of him. But because the impossible had happened. Simon had said sorry. And if that could happen, who knew what else could?

The sun streamed through the window warming the table between them.

Doreen had decided to live.

Tarryn Meaker

Tarryn was born in Zimbabwe and has done a lot of things since then – mostly unexpected. She's a single parent of three children and works as a Story Producer for a large NGO. She'd rather be writing novels (or being a ballerina, but unfortunately she's too big and old for that).

Helen Jo

1.
Paper Napkins

My mother does not have dementia. But she wishes she did. She yearns for the blank, the absence: of responsibility, of action, of effort. Of decisions. What to keep. What to let go of, forever.

My mother is a packrat. A relative of a hoarder, but keeping up appearances: to strangers, her house simply looks overdecorated. You have to open the closets, the drawers, to see what is going on. The hundreds of empty glass jars stored high up on her kitchen shelves. The walk-in closet in her bedroom stuffed with clothes, hangers crammed so close together it's difficult to select a blouse to wear. Most of the clothes still have tags, recording the bargain price she paid at Ross, T.J. Max, Marshalls. Shopping is the only activity she truly enjoys. Every store presents her with a challenge: finding the items she will purchase, discovering them on her slow transits of women's wear and home goods as though these objects were hidden for her intentionally, like Easter eggs.

My mother is 94 and is selling her house. Everything must go. I was excited to hear that her neighbors -- who for years have carried up the mail from her mailbox and mowed her lawn and looked after everything while she was away visiting one of us -- were having a clothes drive. Their minister was heading to Jamaica and needed shirts, tee shirts and short-sleeved button-downs. My mother had dozens, new with tags. But my mother never gives anything away.

Why won't she donate these shirts she will never wear to the neighbors, to their minister, for the Jamaicans who have suffered a hurricane? She has no answers. The more persuasively the question is framed, the more furious she becomes.

My mother has asked me to help her put her house on the market for each of the past three years. Each time, I've set aside two weeks to help her, but she hasn't let me get rid of a single thing. Last year I spent three days emptying the storage barn in her back yard. I took out all the boxes she'd brought from her old house, the house in New York where I grew up, the boxes she moved to Alabama and never opened. We opened every box and wrote a list of what it contained. I threw out the actual garbage -- broken glass, wadded-up twenty-year-old newspapers -- then put everything back inside the barn.

My mother has accumulated hundreds of packages of decorative paper napkins, for dinner parties or hosting bridge, most stored in an old cherry-wood secretary. All its drawers are stuffed with napkins. Some packs are open and have been partly used, but most are intact. Some are quite beautiful: woven of paper that feels like cloth, printed with butterflies lifted from a Japanese screen.

My aunt would like some of her napkins. My mother won't give her any. "I'm giving Nanette the dining room rug," she says.

"But why not give her some napkins?"

"The man is going to sell everything." This is a man from church that Nanette found to hold an estate sale after my mother's house has sold.

"You'll get maybe ten cents for them!"

"Sharon!" She gave me a name she could hiss. "I am *not* giving them away."

My mother's house looks better after half her things are taken out. There is so much in it -- large abstract paintings, candlesticks, vases, vases, vases full of artificial flowers (good ones -- roses that look real, and fanciful blooms that don't look real at all but are lovely extrapolations of what flowers could be), table lamps, sofas loaded with dozens of pillows (leaving little room to sit), small tables holding candles or more vases.

On the mantel in the living room, lit by a spotlight, is a decorative plate a foot and a half in diameter. It's a picture of zebras mating; the one in back has thrown his foreleg over the other as he mounts her.

"Why do you have a picture of fucking zebras?" I ask.

"Because I like it."

I realize that my mother thinks I mean, *fucking zebras* as in, *Why do you have a picture of zebras, of all things?* "But they're mating. You have a picture of zebras mating on your wall."

"Really? I don't think so." The plate has hung there for years, but she has no idea what the zebras in the spotlight are doing.

2.
Happy Hour

My mother would burst into my room without knocking. "It's 5 o'clock." She was sixty years old, or seventy-eight, or ninety-four, though at ninety-four her entrance was slower. She had to balance on her walker and lean over carefully to reach the doorknob. She no longer had the strength to shove the door open wide. Now she turned the knob and gave a frail push, opening just enough of a crack to make her pronouncement. "It's five o-clock." Her voice never lost its command. Whatever I was doing at that moment, I stopped. I poured her bourbon and my wine and carried our glasses onto the patio, to her chair that nervously rocked, mine that held still. We toasted to the only thing we had in common. "Cheers," she said. "Skol," I said. *Skol*, because my father, who died so long ago I never had the chance to get drunk with him, was Norwegian.

Sometimes she put on red lipstick for our happy hour, or accented her nightgown with a matching bright scarf. Sometimes she changed her clothes, just as she used to change out of her nightgown for my father shortly before he was expected to appear at five or six or seven o'clock. He always called and asked if she needed anything from the grocery store on his way home. That's how she knew to get dressed. She applied her make-up. She carefully placed her wig, a wig that shaped her head into a large firm hair-sprayed bubble. Then she clipped on earrings encrusted with fake jewels, clip-ons so heavy she'd have felt them wagging her ears with every movement of her head, and in high heels, she walked to the overstuffed white chairs where they would have their cocktails, waiting to be waited upon. My father mixed the drinks. It wasn't anything like those old commercials where the wife cheerfully greets her husband at the door with an ice-cold martini.

From the way she screamed at God the night my father died -- she really did believe God would save him, even after my father wasted away to look like a beautiful child, especially his eyes, his eyes became transparent, I want to say transcendent, as though they would open his soul to us, after a lifetime of Norwegian reticence, which he now regretted --

From the way she screamed at God the night my father died, I thought my mother would spend the rest of her days drinking. What else was there for her to do? Soap operas. Bridge, then as her friends died, solitaire. Fox News, when it came along, played 24/7 on her tv. *Fox and Friends*. They really were her friends: when she woke in the middle of the night, they were there to talk her back to sleep. She lived thirty-eight more years. And every day she waited until five, watching the clock the way she'd waited for my father's phone call, then measuring two ounces into the gold-plated jigger. She'd fill her plastic tumbler with cubes of ice, and when the bourbon was gone, she ate the melted bits, crunching them between her dentures like cold nuts.

Sharon Wahl

Sharon Wahl is a writer and documentary film producer living in Tucson, Arizona. Her work has been published in *The Iowa Review* (Tim McGinnis Award), *Chicago Tribune* (Nelson Algren Award Finalist), amongst others. She has an MFA in Creative Writing.

Mother Love

Susan was eight years old when she stumbled on her mother in the outhouse drowning the kittens. The rusty pail, usually used for swilling the yard, was filled to the brim with water. It shimmered darkly, like freshly poured tar. At her mother's feet were two piles of fur. One squirming with pathetic mews that hardly cut the air, so new were they. The other a mangled pile of wetness, still and collapsed with slick pelts sticking each dead kitten to its sibling. Susan judged about six bodies if you included the one her mother had scooped up. It was struggling in her hand, despite only having a few hours' worth of real-life strength in it. Even from the doorway she could see its new eyes slit shut, as if refusing to witness its fate.

Both Susan's hands clamped over her mouth stifling what would have been a scream. A muffled, aching groan escaped instead. Her mother turned swiftly towards the noise; the kitten temporarily relieved from its dying as she looked to see who had disturbed her.

'For Christ's sake, Susan,' she barked. Her surprise at being caught playing God made her angry and embarrassed all at once. Recovering some composure, she dropped the kitten onto the pile of living babies and returned to her role of mother. 'You're supposed to be at school, what the hell are you doing home?' Susan did not look at her. She kept her eyes on the beating pile of fur next to the bucket. All of it made sense now. The family cat, round and fat. Her father scowling, muttering about too many mouths to feed already, every time she slinked in crying for food. Her mother shushing him, saying she will deal with it when the time came. Susan and her brothers had been oblivious to the burgeoning life under their noses.

Her mother moved to stand between Susan and the crush of kittens so she could not see. 'Get out,' she said, 'this is not for you. Get in the house, go on.' But Susan stood her ground. Her heart bent in her chest and, as her hands dropped clenched by her side, she raised her eyes to look at her mother.

'Where's Bella?' she asked, her voice older than its years.

'Bella?' Her mother seemed non plussed, yet her eyes darted around the dimly lit brick walls. She had shut the distressed cat in the house and now worried that Susan may have let her out. Even she could not face seeing the cat discover what she had done.

'Bella, the mamma cat,' Susan said, even though she knew her mother understood exactly who she meant. Her mother flinched.

'Susan, you need to go inside *now*,' she said. 'I'll be in straight away and I will explain.' But Susan stayed and, unclenching her fists, she joined her mother in the gloom of the outhouse, leaving a sharp shaft of spring light with swirling dust behind her. Holding her mother's gaze Susan walked slowly towards the bucket of water, now still as a mirror. As if sensing another, less malevolent presence, the three kittens raised their shrilling to tiny wails. Susan sensed rather than saw them, felt them squirming and blindly reaching for safety. Her mother held her at bay by putting out her outstretched palm like a traffic policeman. 'Do as I say, Susan. This is nothing to do with you. I'm sorry you had to see this, but it needs to be done.'

Susan made to sidestep her mother's hand and it was in this moment of defiance things unravelled. Her mother's warning hand suddenly rose and turned into a hitting hand. She sprang at her daughter, striking her smartly across her face to stop her in her tracks. The clipped sound of the slap was quickly swallowed by the shadows.

Neither of them seemed to be breathing.

Even the kittens were silent.

Unlike her brothers, Susan had rarely been struck by either of her parents, and certainly not like this. Her shock made her falter in her mission. Her mother, shaking herself free from the tableaux, reached for her daughter's arm to pull her in to console, apologise, erase. But ignoring both her mother's endeavours and the pink smarting on her cheek, she deftly bent behind her mother's legs and scooped up two kittens in one hand, then the third in her other. She clutched them to her chest holding them tightly. Their keening returned but was muffled now as she pressed them into the wool of her cardigan. She could feel their pitiful hearts beating against her own, the thrumming giving courage and a righteous path. Susan backed away from her mother and nudged the water in the bucket, the ripples sending the tiniest amount over its side. Looking down she had an overwhelming need to destroy her mother's weapon of choice. Balancing on one leg, she lunged at the bucket with her foot. There was a clash as the metal hit the floor; it's ringing dulled by the weight of water that swilled every which way. The gush picked up the three dead kittens in its flow. It bore them further into the darkness of the outhouse, leaving them to settle in a puddle of discarded water, slowly seeping through the brick floor. Both Susan and her mother stared at the ragged heaps of clagged and twisted fur. Unrecognisable.

Susan was the first to move.

Turning her back, she made for the sunlit doorway, kittens calmer now against her chest. As she crossed the yard, she cupped the three curled bodies with one hand and reached for the back door.

Her mother watched her from where she had been left. Watched as the door opened inward. Watched Bella frantically jump up at Susan's legs, sensing her babies and wanting them close. Watched Susan lower the three kittens gently to their waiting mother. Watched, until the door swung shut with a soft click.

Jayne Stead
Having completed her MA in Creative Writing Jayne has embarked on an MFA to complete her collection of short stories. She captures the smaller vignettes of life, turning them into stories that shed light on class, middlescence and the complexities of being a mother.

Saltbush

We're all made of dust, our Gran would say. Not in a God sort of way, though we'd sometimes catch her throwing salt at the devil when she spilt the shaker on the table. We'd taken in the desert, she said. It was moving inside us. Egg timers, every one of us. Stop in that handstand too long and the sand will run right to your brain. That was our Gran. Always looking out for us.

You won't find her buried round back of the church. She was a fay-ta-list. She taught us that word and said if we had any sense, we'd be one too. She wanted her ashes scattered down the main street of town. We did it early one morning, while our Dad stood watch. He didn't think our neighbours would understand, but he kept his promise all the same. We watched her drift away, into the dust that got harder to shift each year. We didn't say much, but as we left our Dad took off his mask and breathed in deep.

Our Gran was the last to die in that town, but you won't dig up a plaque to her. You will dig up a lot of masks. The ones that haven't rotted, that is. Our Dad said the sand is a natural dess-i-cant. It keeps things the way they were. But it won't tell you who we were, or how we used the things you find here, the way we lived. The desert was moving in, taking back what belonged to it, and all we had to meet it with were brooms and masks. We were always going to lose, but we put up a pretty good fight.

That wasn't all we had, that was a bit of a lie. Our Dad worked in the mine until it shut down, and sometimes he'd bring home chunks of fool's gold. Iron py-rite, they call it. It's not real, though it might be worth something now, if you find any in what's left of our house. But it glitters for real. Our Dad would set the rock on the sideboard, and our Gran would use it to prop open the back door when she went to water the pumpkins. We'd hang at the kitchen table and watch it catch the sun. We weren't allowed out much anymore, even with masks on, so we sat and watched it shine on the porch, and fancied it lit the way to a river deep underground, where the water ran gold. Our Dad would open a beer and drag his chair up to ours. He'd tell us about the saltbush they planted at the mine, to re-gen-a-rate the land. Saltbush can live pretty much anywhere. It's all over the desert. You can even eat it. Our Gran said a bad word we weren't allowed to repeat every time our Dad brought a bunch home, but she'd still fry it up with the vegetables. The saltbush stops the dunes from moving, and for a while they thought it would stop the wind lifting the top sand and carrying it across town. But the desert is patient, our Gran would say – it'd come for us in time. Soon enough, the back door stayed shut for good. The windows too. The bedroom rug felt like sandpaper, and our Dad would spend the afternoons bent over a dustpan and brush, sweeping up the dirt that streaked across the lounge room floor.

Our Dad wouldn't hear a word against the mine. It gave us the where-with-all to get out while the getting was good, he'd say, when our Gran would square up to him about it. She came from a farming family, and thought she knew how to work the land. But that was a long time ago, in a place much colder than this. A place with no sand and no masks, where your breath would cloud in front of you. We used to think that was why she'd get up early to wash the sheets and hang them on the line, with her woollen scarf wrapped around her face. There are no clouds in the desert, so the heat vanishes overnight. We thought the cold morning air reminded her of that home, the one she left behind. When we asked her, she laughed and told us that hanging the sheets out in the cold made them whiter. But the sand took care of that too. Our Gran would drag the sheets off the line and shake them at our Dad, pointing at the patterns the red dust had made, turning our bedsheets into roadmaps.

Do you come from a cold place? We read that in some places the soil never thaws. Per-ma-frost, they call it. We used to put on our masks and take our lunchboxes and our thermos and bike to the edge of town. We'd sit beneath the welcome sign that said population 1,472. That was a bit of a lie – a lot of people moved away before the end. We'd sneak our masks down and eat peanut butter sandwiches and take turns sipping hot chocolate from the thermos, looking out at red nothing, as far as we could see. Do you look out at white nothing? We read that no trees grow in frozen soil, but we saw a picture of moss all over the ground. Do you eat moss like we eat saltbush?

If you want to know our names, you'll find them scratched under the big wooden table in the kitchen. If it survived, that is. We hid under there one night when our Dad was mad at us and scratched our names in the wood with a cheese knife. When our Gran found us, she spelt out our Mum's name so we could put it next to ours. We don't know what happened to our Mum. When you're older, our Gran would say, when we asked. Our Dad would say our Mum loved us very much, then he'd look out the window, as if he expected to see her out front. Maybe you'll find out what happened. Maybe you'll find one of the runners she made on the table. But a student from a big city university once told us that fabric is quick to de-te-ri-o-rate, so the runners may be dust by the time you get here.

The student came to stay with us, close to the end. It was the first time we heard the word re-lo-ca-shun. They sent people to town to ask us how we felt about it. We weren't sure what they were planning to do when they found out we felt bad. It wasn't the student's fault. She was an assistant, studying an-thro-po-lo-gy. Our Dad pointed to where she lived on the map pinned on our bedroom wall. It might still be there. The map, that is. The big city might still be there too, but you'd know more about that than we do. The student said her school had fifteen thousand pupils. Ours had forty. We're an aging population, our Dad said, and he pointed at her notebook and told her to write that down. We gave her a piece of fool's gold. She said she'd use it as a paperweight, for her dis-er-ta-shun. Maybe that's how you'll find us. You'll read her paper, or see our rock in a museum somewhere, and you'll follow the pieces and they'll lead you here.

Do you still have museums? Our Dad took us to one once, to look at fossils. That was where we learnt about arch-e-o-lo-gists. They dig things up and put them together and make a story about what life used to be like. Our Dad bought us a kit from the gift shop to make our own fossils. Our Gran helped us mix the plaster and we poured it into the casts that came in the box. We collected leaves and twigs from out back and made spirals out of the pumpkin seeds our Gran had set to dry on the windowsill. They're not real fossils, though. If you find them in our bedroom cupboard, we wouldn't want you to get the wrong idea.

Maybe you'll pass through here one day and see telegraph poles sticking up through the sand, like bleached old bones. Our neighbours are making a time capsule, but the student who stayed with us said that wasn't a good idea. She said it might give future gen-a-ray-shuns the wrong idea about what things were important to us. It might give them the wrong idea about things that weren't even from our time. Like De Mille, our Gran snorted. Do you still have movies? Cecil B DeMille was a man who made movies, and one time he made this giant set of Ancient Egypt in the desert, and left it there for the sand to cover. It's not really Ancient Egypt, but maybe someday someone like you will think it is, and that's how lies get started. We're not going to make a time capsule. We'll leave things as they lay, and trust you to do the work.

We can't take everything with us, but that leaves more for you to dig up. The student who stayed with us talked about something called a pot-latch. That's where you give away your things and it makes you look richer. Our Gran said it made no sense, but she still gave her stuff away before she died. Di-vest-ing, she called it. She gave us her collection of crystal animals. We put them on the desk in our bedroom and they'd turn all sorts of colours in the morning sun. We'd never give those away. We gave away our bikes though. The town was splitting up, so we sent our stuff in as many directions as we could. Maybe in one of those new places, we wouldn't cough behind our masks when we went outside. Maybe we wouldn't need masks at all. Our Dad got mad about the bikes, but it wasn't like we could use them anymore. Besides, he was the one who'd taken off his mask that morning and breathed in the ashes of our Gran. He knew how it worked.

Our Dad says we have to go soon. He's gone outside to pack the car. There's a big blue tarp sitting in the driveway. He'll tie what doesn't fit in the boot onto the roof rack and cover it with the tarp, so we don't take the desert with us. Our Gran would have called him su-per-sti-shus, but she would have been out there anyway, packing our stuff right beside him.

We're going to put this in the biscuit tin our Gran used to keep old receipts in. It has a picture of a lady with a bustle dress on it, but that's not what we wore. That's a re-pro-duck-shun of an old painting. We don't know what time that dress belongs to, it's just a thing we used to do – put pictures of old things on new things. We don't know whether you'll get this. We should have asked that anth-ro-po-lo-gist what to do. But if we had, could she have told us if you'd be able to read what we wrote? Do you speak our language? At the museum, we learnt the Ancient Egyptians wrote with pictures called hy-ro-gli-fix, and no one knew how to read them until someone found a stone that had the same message written in different languages. The pictures were next to a language someone else knew how to read, and that was the key. We wish we had a key, but we don't know what languages will come between you and us. We hope ours lives long enough for you to understand us. If it doesn't, that's okay. We were dust long before you were born, but here we are, beneath the saltbush, moving through the desert, waiting for you to drop your mask and breathe us in.

Amanda Hildebrandt

Amanda Hildebrandt is a published writer and academic. Her most ambitious project to date has been the completion of a PhD thesis on flight attendant uniforms. Amanda's fiction has won and placed in several awards. *Saltbush* was first published in *Mslexia*.

Say Hello to Yama

(Based on actual events)

Content Warning: This story is based on devastating landslides in December 2022 which killed 31 people. It, therefore, deals with sensitive issues and contains racially-charged dialogue.

'Every year, individuals and communities are affected by natural disasters [and] will experience feelings of anxiety, sadness, hopelessness, fatigue, irritability or anger, as well as difficulty sleeping.'

Professor (Adj) Dato' Dr. Andrew Mohanraj

Oh my!

A pewter grey sky with stunning mandarin clouds criss-crossing throughout was more than the necessary drama in what promised to be the tail end of two weeks of floods and the threat of landslides. Squatting behind the village mosque in Kampung Sungai Tua, I looked out at the river. With a single glance, I knew that it was logs of *cengal* that floated downstream. Maybe, the day would come when I'd see His – I refused to say my husband's name; it was best to use pronouns, instead – body floating among the logs.

Because of Him, we ran for our lives.

Because of Him, we lived as one of the hard-core poor.

Because of Him, we'd pretended to be part of a religion we weren't born into.

I stood up and arranged the folds of my kaftan and hijab. Holding the Tupperware containing durians close, I was eager to eavesdrop on the *cakap-cakap* by the water pump. All the way to this gossip session, I lamented as to how my once-charmed life had come to this.

***

The gunpowder grey sky was punctuated by twinkling stars the night He received a phone call from the *ah long*. The loan shark threatened grievous bodily harm if He didn't settle his debts as soon as possible. A shiny new *parang* was left outside our front door the next day. Picking up the machete, He shivered upon opening the attached note which read as follows: 'U R Next.'

Within twenty-four hours, we abandoned our lives, boarded the next available bus out of Alor Setar and got off when it stopped outside a mosque in the middle of nowhere. We remained silent when Wahab, the *penghulu* of Kampung Sungai Tua and pseudo-Imam, assuming we were Muslims, saw it as his moral duty to offer us shelter.

"Our sister, Kak Tom, has a small place next to her house. You can stay there."

As we lay on the mat spread out on the floor that first night in our new home, He turned to me and whispered, "Just imagine. From being Ricky, I'm now Ahmad. And you, from Bhoomi, you're now Putri. So easy."

I should have said something, but I didn't know what to say.

I followed Him on his second visit to what the villagers now called 'The Hut'. A forest ranger named Boon Teong explained that it was once a temporary shelter for Rohingya women. They waited for middle men who promised them safe passage to their menfolk in Sumatra and beyond. Instead, they were shipped off to *mamasans* in the city brothels. Once this prostitution and human trafficking ring was busted, the villagers used The Hut as a place to rest whenever they went in search of herbs and other medicinal plants.

"I've got work," He whispered, one day about four months after we'd first arrived. "Some people need to clear the jungle. Use the land to create a latex clone forest farm."

"A what?"

"It's about rubber trees."

"Who said?" Nothing was mentioned about this during the latest *cakap-cakap*.

"Remember Boon Teong? He guessed that I am actually Chinese."

"How?"

"I don't know." He looked at the kettle with boiling water bubbling away.

"This is dangerous."

"No lah." He picked up the *parang* and started to sharpen it. "This will protect us. He wants to help me get extra money to pay off the *ah long* and go home."

"He knows about the *ah long*?" I lifted the kettle off the stove and began to make his *teh tarik*.

"Aiya, no need to think so much, okay?"

He raised his voice. Instinctively, I pulled the ends of my sleeves to hide the fading bruises on my forearm. Had I the courage, I would have asked Him, 'How does that *parang* help you?'

The day the government changed a year later, supposedly for the better, we had a marbled sky of bright blue with streaks of dull grey. The forest reserve upstream had been cleared. At one thousand metres above sea level, it was what experts called a high hill dipterocarp forest and was deemed environmentally sensitive.

In Kampung Sungai Tua, this called for a gathering – far more serious than the usual *cakap-cakap* – inside the school hall.

Dispensing with preliminaries, Wahab called the meeting to order.

"There are logging activities upstream. Do any of you know anything about this?"

I glanced at Him who was looking straight ahead.

"It's like this," Wahab said. "Put a hen and a few chicks on some grass. Pour a drum of water on them and they will run here, there and everywhere, but the grass will absorb the water. Now, you take away the grass and make it a cement floor. Put the same hen and chicks there. Throw water and what happens? They will be washed away."

Shoulders started to droop.

"What do you think will happen to us when there's heavy rain now? We'll be like those chickens. We will be washed away."

Everyone hung their head low.

Cakap-cakap

"What happened to the latex clone forest?"

"Not enough money. New company sold the land to an operator of a durian orchard."

"Durian? Our kind of soil, can or not?"

"Sure can. If anything happens, no one will blame us."

"Why, ah?"

"Wahab said because the company got director who is *krabat*. You know lah, with royalty, everything will be okay."

"Ya lah."

The day the trees were completely uprooted for the durian orchard, the sky was ash grey without a single streak of silver. The rays of the sun shone on the spot where a reservoir was created to irrigate the orchard. Reservoir was too posh a word, perhaps, to describe what was nothing more than a gigantic hole in the ground. Soon, previously water-logged plots of flat paddy land were mud-logged testaments that their source of irrigation had become unsuitable for cultivating paddy.

"How could this have happened?"

"Don't ask so many questions, Bhoomi." He opened the leather pouch and counted the notes inside, then sipped on the tumbler of fermented rice called *tuak*.

"This is not good. The Gods will be angry. Then how? Yama will come."

"You and your Yama. No need to bring all this Hindu-Bindu gods." Shivering, he showed his disgust for my faith by adding, "Eeee...."

I looked away. Something wasn't right. I could feel it. It was also the moment when I first had an inkling that there would come a time when I would need to gather my wits about me.

Life bumbled along until the day I couldn't see the sky through the fat raindrops. As the twilight hour began, He rushed into our space.

"I saw him, Bhoomi."

"Who?"

"Him." When I stared, perplexed, he shook his hands in front of him, frustrated. "The *ah long*."

"W-h-a-?" I cleared my throat.

"Boon Teong brought him to the durian orchard. This *ah long* fellow is his friend lah! Die-die, I tell you."

As I watched him gather his things into a plastic bag – one shirt, a pair of trousers, phone charger and toiletries – it dawned on me. He was packing for one.

"What about me?"

He stopped. Stood up and held my shoulders.

"I will go first. Pay this *ah long* fellow." Suddenly, he started hitting his head with his palm. "Alamak! I forgot the pouch." He began pacing. "It's in The Hut. I go back there to get money." One more squeeze of my shoulders and he added, "But I will leave some money there for you. Five hundred ringgit."

The next thing I knew, He was gone.

I stood there, in the middle of our one hundred square feet dwelling place for the past five years, accepting my reality for the first time ever. I had married a self-centred, good-for-nothing who didn't care if I lived or died.

The fading inky blue sky didn't help to light my path to The Hut. If it had, I could have been forewarned. As it transpired, it was Boon Teong's left hand I saw first when I stepped into The Hut. It was minus the ring finger. It seemed, He said months ago, Boon Teong had lost it at an irritated goldsmith's shop.

The next thing I saw was the leather pouch.

"Ah, there you are. There is a lot of money here. Five thousand lah. That Ricky made a lot, ah?"

For a long while, I watched him.

"Please, give me my money. My husband's money."

"Your husband?" He sniggered. "My friend saw him the other day. My friend, ah, not so kind one, you know. And money still here, what? Maybe… you know."

I held my breath.

"Now, all alone." We made eye contact then. A brief encounter – one that left me certain of what he was implying.

I tried to grab the pouch from him.

"Ah, ah, ah," the Boon Teong deflected. "Tell you what. Here," he said, handing the pouch to me. "Take it."

He did not let go, though, when I put my hand on the pouch.

"I want something in return."

I should have let go of the pouch then. But I needed the money.

When I couldn't admit to myself what happened next, how was anyone going to believe a word I said?

"Ah," Boon Teong said when it was over. "Here. Five hundred ringgit. I will keep the rest. Keep safe for you." Zipping his pants, he said, "Come back next Wednesday, okay?"

With each step back down the hill, I recited a mantra to the spirits watching and begged for forgiveness for defiling their space.

A thousand curses unto Him. He'd taken the *parang* with Him and I had nothing but my wits to defend myself. I heard the rumble and opened my eyes. Peeping through the gaps in wood, the sky was a canopy of velvety black. Turning my back to the apology for a door hanging off its hinges, I opened the pill box and dropped the tablets into the plastic bottle of fermented rice wine. Watching the effervescence, I prayed that the three hundred ringgit I'd paid for the pills be worth every sen. The faith healer promised that three pills were enough to knock out an elephant.

I heard their words.

"How much? Hundred?"

"No lah. No need so much. Fifty each enough. This orang kampung only. Give this durian also enough already."

The bastard meant to short change me. There was only one thing to do. I slipped all the pills into the jug making it three pills each for three lecherous souls. I flung open the door. Boon Teong turned, saw me holding out the jug and three tumblers. Greedy, they drank every drop and fell face down into the mud.

***

Cakap-cakap.

"Putri, you heard or not, what happened?"

"What?"

"Two Chinaman. One Malay fellow. Died lah."

"Oh."

"Wahab found them near The Hut. But all hush-hush because the Malay fellow is *krabat*."

"Oh... You want? Durian?"

"Wah! Delicious."

Under the fading dawn sky, chequered shades of pale yellow and powder blue, I squatted next to the logs by the river. I pulled the pouch from its hiding place and put it into the plastic bag I brought back from *cakap-cakap,* I stood up. At that very moment, a body floated past. It was bloated, caked in mud, hands akimbo and fingers splayed. The ring finger on the right hand was missing.

"Say Hello to Yama."

References:

Mohanraj, A. (2023, January 3). Dealing with the psychological trauma of disasters. *The Star Online*. Retrieved in January 2023 from www.thestar.com.my/lifestyle/health/matters-of-the-mind/2022/01/03/dealing-with-the-psychological-trauma-of-disasters

---

Aneeta Sundararaj

Aneeta Sundararaj is an award-winning short story writer who developed a website called *How to Tell a Great Story*. Her work has been featured in many publications. Her bestselling novel, *The Age of Smiling Secrets* was shortlisted for the Book Award in Malaysia.

Some Life, This

I've seen some weird stuff working as a night receptionist in this motel in Kings Cross. One night these four guys came in at midnight and they wanted the room until 7am to play cards. Straight away my mind started working and I thought, right if I could get them out before 6am, then, ah, they wouldn't have used the beds. It would just be beer cans and emptying ashtrays and a quick vacuum. Then I could spray some air freshener around and keep the money. I told the guy who was doing all the talking that, hey, we didn't do that here but if they could get out by six, well, I could do them a favour and let them have the room for one hundred and twenty, and they agreed and I was like, in my mind, high fiving myself. I had made one hundred and twenty, because I like a bet and it was my stake for the next couple of days.

I started out as the evening guy, That's what the manager called me. He said,

'You're going to be the evening guy.'

I had worked with him before, he was shifty but that was Kings Cross, shifty.

I said to him 'Brad, 'I'll do whatever the hell you want. You know me. I can do it easy.'

He said,

'You've got working experience here in The Cross, you know what goes on. I can trust you not to let the room to people who are going to trash it. No guys bringing in working girls from the street, that kind of thing.'

'Right, right, of course not. I know the kind of trouble that can cause and stuff, you know, I've worked a few places in the area and...'

'Yes, that's why I'm choosing you. It can be a different world here sometimes.'

'I totally agree, gee, I could tell you some stories to Brad. I know you got some stories too.'

'Keith will train you. You'll only probably need one night. Keith is thorough, so listen to him, no shortcuts.'

I turned up the next afternoon at three on the dot. Keith shook my hand. He was wearing a black and white checked shirt, a black tie, black pants and he wore steel-rimmed glasses, had flowing grey hair down past his collar and he said,

'Welcome aboard the mad house.'

I thought that was funny and that we would get along fine and we did. Like Brad said, he was a thorough guy. He'd typed out a list of stuff to do on the shift numbered one to thirty. I thought I'd do about ten of them, total. I had used the front office computer system before, so he couldn't teach me anything there. It was getting the rooms down. The room types I mean. You know twin beds, double bed, single, queen beds, how many fold-up beds did the place have? How many people maximum allowed in the room and so on and so forth. There was a chart anyway, so if I got stuck, I would look at the chart, it wasn't rocket science. The same thing with the room rates, there was a chart, you followed it.

One time this guy came in and he ranted and raved about being ripped off by a street girl, a working girl. He was saying this bitch and that bitch and so on. I hated it with these guys. They came to Kings Cross to pick up a working girl and expected things to go smoothly, like buying a shirt in Kmart or something. He asked me to call him an escort. I told him there was a Yellow Pages in the room.

'Look it up yourself.'

'Great service,' he said.

Screw you, I thought.

The agency call came through and I put it through to his room. An hour later the girl arrived and I said to her,

'Be careful with this guy, he's a dick.'

She only smiled and nodded, which is fine, she was the expert, not me.

Half an hour later I heard screams in the stairwell and she burst through the door into the reception area, and yelled, 'he cut me, he cut me,' and I could see blood on her face and my heart started beating through my chest like I was a racehorse or something. I opened the hatch at the end of the desk and dragged her in by the arm. I could see it wasn't a bad cut, not deep. We had an arm robbery button (most motels in the area did) and I pressed it and a few minutes later the local detectives came charging in the door (the cop shop was about three minute's walk away) and I said, '303, he's in 303, he cut her.' They opened the stairwell door and the guy who had cut the girl rushed out holding a damn pocket knife out in front of him. They wrestled him to the floor right in front of me. I need blood money, I thought. I was skimping the till a bit so I guess I was getting it but hell. What a night.

Three months into the gig. It was 11.30 and I was dying to go home but the night guy who worked from 11pm to 7am hadn't turned up. The motel was small time, with no backups. I mean there were only thirty rooms in the whole place. I called Brad and told him and he said,

'Can you, do it?'

'The whole shift?'

'Yeah.'

'I guess but er...'

'I'll pay you cash in the morning.'

'Two hundred.'

'One-fifty.'

'Alright, I'll do it,' I said and that's how I became the night guy on a permanent basis.

The other thing that happened is that when I got paid in the morning, Brad didn't go to the motel safe. We had safety deposit boxes for the guests, for their passports, cash and travellers' cheques and stuff. The guest had one key, we had the other but Brad had both keys. He went to one of the safety deposit boxes and opened it with the keys. I saw there were thousands of dollars in there and I thought, shit, what's that for but said nothing.

I'm the night guy I told a few people. I got to know a few of the street girls who worked close to the front door. I couldn't smoke inside and like I said, there were only thirty rooms, it wasn't busy. I stood or sat on the front stoop and smoked and drank coke and watched the world, the mad world of Kings Cross go back and forth in front of me. The suburban mums and dads out for a drag show and a few drinks. The suburban boys and girls up for anything in the clubs and bars all around Darlinghurst Road—the dirty-half-mile. The spruikers yelled and tried to cajole people into their strip clubs while they laughed, and smoked cigarettes, and said anything to get people inside. I saw fist fights and cowardly bashings and drunk girls who had made a mess of their mascara and themselves. The boys arm in arm singing Cold Chisel songs. Stories, stories everywhere.

A few nights ago, a middle-aged guy running to fat and with a comb-over of black hair saw me standing there, smoking and he whispered to me,

'Can I get a girl, bring her into your motel.'

He looked harmless enough. I called Beccy and she came by in about ten minutes and I introduced them to each other and upstairs they went and they were back down in about fifteen minutes. Wham bam.

'Easy money,' I said to Beccy, and she laughed.

Present day and life is getting a bit rough for me. I owe a bit of money to a local guy, a loan shark. Name of Bobby Grigg. I couldn't get the money together so I made a deal with him to run girls out of the motel on my night shift. I recruited Tracy and another girl Sharon and Bobby Grigg has two girls of his own. It's got out of control. I have to bloody clean the four rooms before Brad arrives in the morning. It is doing my head in. I keep thinking about that money in the safety box. I need the steady income from the job and I still gamble like mad. I have not much else to live for.

Then, one morning, Brad comes in and the morning receptionist girl doesn't show up. I know something's up and Brad says to me,

'I know what you're doing.'

'Huh?'

'You're checking people in, they leave early and you clean the rooms and keep the cash.'

He's kind of right.

'It has to stop,' he says

'Yeah, Brad, sorry, it will, it will.'

'You need money to get you by.'

'You're sacking me?'

'You get three days' notice according to the award, you're lucky to get that.'

'Yeah, sorry Brad, I know you...'

'Save it, you're putting all our jobs at risk.'

What's that bloody stash you got in the safety deposit box I want to say but don't. I'm not too sure what I'll do. I have about three hundred in cash. I wander home along Macleay Street to my little bachelor unit in Potts Point, grab a few hours of sleep, then shower and out the door to the TAB in the Crest Hotel Arcade. I win about a thousand dollars and feel pretty great but I owe Bobby Grigg way more than that. The thousand would only cover about a third of the debt and he kills me with interest even after I let the girls use the rooms.

I walk to the supermarket and buy a heap of groceries and toilet paper and a few USB sticks and some A4 paper and some little chocolate toys, they call them Kinder Surprise. I walk along Macleay Street to Orwell Street, and then cut down a little lane and into a backyard, knock on the door of the little garden flat. Beccy answers, and her eyes are little black pins, she must have shot up earlier. I say to her,

'Hello love, I got you some groceries and toilet paper and stuff, you need some money for the rent or something like that, anything?'

'Rent's due today, bloody landlord is coming round later, I don't...'

'Yep, sweet, Beccy, I knew that, here's six hundred,' I say and hand her the cash. I'll stay around until he gets here, make sure he gets paid. Be alright, huh.'

'Yeah, course, thanks, Stuart. God, Jesus, you're a lifesaver.'

'How's little Chloe, I got some little chocolate toys for her and...'

'Go, go, she's in her room, she loves you mate, loves you...don't know what we'd do without you,' she says and she's all over the shop and I get scared for Chloe, that one day Beccy will overdose. But what can you do?

Sean O'Leary

Sean O'Leary is a writer from Melbourne, Australia. He has published five short story collections, four novels and over forty individual short stories in literary magazines. He likes to walk all over the face of the Earth, write like a demon and take photos like a madman.

Sweetheart

(Circa 1970)

In the bedroom of the small sea cottage far from home, with beams of morning light through the curtain lace making strange shapes of rose gold on the pinewood floor, Elijah Walton Nathaniel Jennings—fine rancher, good husband, better father than son, a man of few words over his morning coffee or an evening sunset but teller of fantastical tales if anywhere near a wood fire, and never happier than when on a horse just riding around staring at things—sat alone in the corner in a ladder-back chair, pointing a gun at his temple.

He held his breath. He pressed the muzzle against his skin. He counted one, two, three . . . and then winced.

No, you can't wince.

Waiting to try again, he bided the time humming a tune in his head before stopping. He couldn't remember the rest. He twitched his facial muscles to ward off an itch. He tried a different tune.

He rolled his eyes around now in their sockets, scanning the room. He could see the smallest things. The nail in the wall where a picture once hung. A glint of light through the keyhole. A beetle crawling under the door, waddling along as if it had all the time in the world. Stopping now to investigate a black speck of something. Working it now with its antennae. Disappearing now into a crack in the boardjoinings. And there, just off to the left beneath the bed, a piece of Tommy's Legos tangled in a dust bunny. By the nightstand, a shred of red ribbon tightly curled as if it'd just been run across a scissor blade. The pen cap he'd been looking for. A shard of broken glass from the night before.

He dug the muzzle in deeper.

It hurt.

He thought about home. And the mountains. And his friend, the blue star living above the field behind the shed on those darkest of nights, blinking secret messages in Morse code. He thought about hard work. The sound his saddle made rubbing against his jeans in the early morning cold. His boots dusted in hoarfrost. The silence of snowfall. He thought about being a boy again when he used to wrap his savings up in an old flannel shirt, making neat little tucks and folds, then hiding the tidy bundle high up in his bedroom closet. Till he needed it someday. He thought about his grandfather too—a full-blooded Shoshone Indian—and soon there he was turning out one of the workhorses. Shutting the screen door behind him without making a sound on a midsummer's eve. Laying trout in a creel, like he was putting them to bed for a rest after a good fight. Coaxing sparks from a campfire deep into the night with the wave of a hand to take their place among the stars.

He thought about that late afternoon down by the road, three days after Grandfather died, when he spotted a two-headed eagle tearing a mouse apart between its two beaks. Deeming it a sign of something.

And seeing the lone coyote at the cattle fence come twilight and not shooting. Just watching it work its way across the meadow for the longest time. Then, it reaching the edge and looking back at him before disappearing into the foothills in a soft rain.

He thought about stormy days spent sitting in the barn, smelling the warm smell of horses and the rain beating down on the corrugated tin roof as if heaven itself had let loose a stampede of tiny angel horses and looking out and watching all the sky colors change, making way for the tiny angel horses to go back up.

He backed his head off the gun a moment as if pausing a telephone call, listening. But it was all too far gone now.

Then got right back at it.

Thinking about Kim now and that first day they met back in high school in Bishop, California. It was 1957. He was on the track field practicing. And there she was too straddling the blocks in a streak of spring sun just before a race. Her lean legs tight as a bow. And eyes so dark and liquid you'd think they'd spill right out of their orbits if it wasn't for those high cheekbones damming them in.

He thought about their first date too that Saturday night so long ago. *Old Yeller* at the drive-in in his dad's truck. He cried at the end, but she didn't. He said he'd known all along the dog was going to die. But she swore there was a version of the movie out there where he didn't die. Just depended upon which theater you saw it in. And you couldn't prove her wrong unless you went to all the theaters in all the countries in all the world.

And afterward, driving along Highway 395 back up to her place, just before town when he turned onto a dirt road. About half a mile in through the desert scrub and blackness of night— just this side of the Milky Way—he found a good spot and parked. He put his hand on her seat back. She looked out the front window and up at the sky. Then after a moment, turned and said her real name was Kimanah and she was Shoshone, too, actually half.

"The top half or the bottom half," he asked?

"Wouldn't you like to know?" she said. Then, "You may kiss me now."

Caused a lump to swell down so deep in his throat, he almost choked.

He then thought about the different sort of lump now swelling in his throat. The lump that hadn't gone away. The lump that kept getting bigger and bigger no matter what the doctors down there had been doing to try to fix it.

"Sweetheart," a voice called from the front room.

He glanced at the closed door out of the corner of his eye. But then looked straight ahead again.

Trying another way now, he slid the barrel up along the side of the cranium where his hair used to be, stopping at what seemed the appropriate place but to no avail. That wasn't right either, he thought. *Perhaps it's best like this*, turning the gun upside down, placing the muzzle up against the roof of his mouth.

"Sweetheart, whatever are you doing in there?"

I'd have to angle it up a smidgen into the brain cavity. He rotated his wrist slightly to see.

"You promised your son you'd take him down to the beach."

And pull the trigger with my thumb. He considered this a moment too.

"And go hunting for Sand crabs."

Yes, I can do that . . .

"Come look, Tommy's got his pail and shovel ready to go."

. . . if I had to do that.

Kimanah called out one last time, "I said, Sweetheart."

Just not today.

He extracted the gun from his mouth, wrapped it up in an old flannel shirt, making neat little tucks and folds, and put the tidy bundle back high up in the closet where it came from.

Then he walked out of the room.

David Landau

David Landau received his Bachelor of Arts in English from The University of California at Berkeley and is an alumnus of the Iowa Writers' Workshop programme. He is a novelist and short story writer. His works can be read in *The Cossack Review*, *580 Split* and more.

Taking Out The Trash

Julie fucking Henderson never takes her bin bags down to the street. Every week they pile up in the hallways, stinking the place up with microwave dinners and cat shit until someone gets so sick of the smell they just drag the rubbish down themselves. No amount of coercion, cajoling, or pleading works for very long; after only a week or two she's back at it, dropping the bags just outside her door. Now bright flames and black smoke pour from her windows, and Lieutenant Deppler finds himself unsurprised that the door to his neighbour's flat is blocked by a flaming pile of trash. Already yellow tongues lick up the walls from the black bags, and their contents smell even worse as they burn.

He had felt a stone drop from his throat to his stomach when the call came into the station. The fire had already spread through half the building and even as he pulled on his suit, he knew it was going to be his half.

Now he stands, visor down and axe in hand, in front of the door 217. Flames coat the wall from floor to ceiling and creep along the carpet and he can feel the heat of it seeping through his jacket. Julie bin-bags Henderson needs his help. Deppler thinks of all the times over the last two and a half years he lost hair and sleep over the menace next door; leaving her cat out on the balcony to yowl for hours; loudly FaceTiming her sister in the middle of the night and practically yelling through their shared wall; the lasagna incident. He feels his blood boiling.

Lieutenant Deppler raises his axe. He swings it at the door.

It sinks into the charred wood, which splinters as he wrenches back. The sudden rush of air feeds the flames and sends them jumping at the newly exposed, unburnt bits. He swings again.

Kicking the fiery bags out of his way the lieutenant enters the room and sees her. Julie Henderson lays face down on her burning carpet, unmoving and exactly where he left her. Deppler moves closer but he already knows what he'll find: bruises around her neck, petechiae of her eyes and face, a fractured skull. Still, he kicks her over, just to make sure. Satisfied, he steps over the body and peers out the glass doors. A set of yellow eyes, overflowing with fear, peer back at him from the balcony. With a smile the lieutenant slides the door open. The cat hisses, back arched, and swipes at Deppler as he grabs the little beast by the scruff of its neck.

Josey Diaz

Josey Diaz is a Creative Writing student at Bath Spa University. A New Jersey native, she currently works at Waterstones and likes to spend her time working out, reading books, and also playing video games – that is when she's not busy writing her silly little stories.

The Footsteps of my Dead Mother

She's here. Again. Fifth night in a row.

Mom's footsteps are the most unique I know. No man nor beast on the planet walks like this.

They have maintained their slow jazzy rhythm even after her burial. It is especially the sound of her favourite brown clogs that wakes me up midnight calling her name. Top quality leather clogs studded with metal buckles along the sole.

Mom loved them. I hated them. Even wanted to hide them at some point because they made her look "disabled." A comment mom rebuked with an unforgettable blow to my head, followed by an order to,

"Apologise to all the disabled people you just offended right now. *Ag. Sies, man.* How could you insult disabled people like that?"

I apologised while dodging a second blow, which was so powerful, it almost tripped her out of her clogs when it missed the back of my head and landed in the air, almost dragging her whole body down to the floor.

It's been three months since we buried mom.

My biggest regret from her funeral is that I contained myself and stayed glued to the mourner's chair while her body descended. I should have acted like they do in those *Mzansi* telenovelas. I should have bellowed, thrown myself to the ground, run to the grave, and thrown myself onto the coffin.

Arg! Sies, maan. I am mad at myself for giving mom such a boring send-off. She was such a phenomenal woman, I should have created drama and sent her off with a BANG!

Nightmares have created the dramatic scenes where real life failed to. My dreams let me know that, in a parallel universe, it was drama at the funeral. I know that in another universe, I threw myself on her coffin and we got buried together and lived happily ever after.

I often hear her clogs walking up and down the passage. I get up knowing mom is in the house and I run to embrace her. It takes a couple of minutes before I realise, she's gone.

Mom is dead. Live with it.

When it happens, I exist somewhere between daydreaming and sleepwalking. I get up feeling her presence heavy in the house. Mom was such a character, even in her death, her presence fills every air particle that surrounds her. It's especially that citrus scent she bathed in.

I follow her footsteps as they leave my bedroom, walk past dad's room, the bathroom, the guest room, now turned auntie's room, all the way to the kitchen.

I enter the kitchen expecting to find mom humming to a latest hit by *Joyous Celebration*, wearing her Jacaranda blue bonnet, her snuggly one-piece nightie and of course, the clogs.

The clogs quadruple and double as church shoes, grocery shoes, go-to-town shoes, cleaning shoes, gardening shoes and sleepers. I know in African culture you are not supposed to see your parents in *that way*, right, but I imagine she wore those clogs even during *the deed*.

I follow to the kitchen and my heart skips when I find no one. The kitchen is "horror empty," where you expect a ghost to jump out from behind the door. The sink is spilling with dishes from the whole of yesterday, and a little bit of the night before where I made more dishes after sneaking up midnight and finishing up any leftover food.

Mom would never. It was mandatory to wash the dishes, dry them and put them away before bed. No compromise. The kitchen must sleep clean. She was right. The ants, cockroaches and flies that accumulated overnight, especially in summer, turned the kitchen into a pit toilet.

When I don't find mom in the kitchen, I do not lose hope. I follow her rhythmic steps to the living room. She's not there. For a while I stare at the corner sofa mom preserved. No one would dare be caught sitting there. Were it possible, she would have carved her name on it and the warning, "SITTERS WILL BE PROSECUTED."

The sofa is next to the coffee table carrying the remote mom dictated. I am still staring at the sofa, hoping that mom will materialise, and we will watch one more Nigerian movie, side by side, mom and daughter, one last time before I finally accept that she's passed on. That would be my closure. I stare at the sofa. My bones are bloody cold, craving the warmth of a mother's embrace.

When mom doesn't materialise, I head to the dining room, my last beacon of hope. The dining room is a little bit dark, lit only by the light from the living room. I am hoping mom is somewhere in there. This is the last shot.

I am just about to enter the dining room when I hear the guest room door open. Auntie disturbs my grieving trip. She is up for her midnight bathroom break. She is a devout water drinker who doesn't touch sugary drinks. I envy her health. Her flat stomach and slim figure are testament to her divorce from sugar. I am jealous of her body.

Embarrassed by my grief, I quickly run to the corner of the dark dining room and sit quiet. I am praying auntie goes straight to her room after her bathroom visit. I don't want a repeat of what happened the last time she woke up and found me in the middle of my midnight grief.

She felt sorry for me, prayed for me, cried with me, comforted me, tucked me in her bed and took a leave from work. She woke up, made breakfast for me, delivered it to my bed, washed my clothes, including my undies, refused to let me do any work in the house, served me the whole day, and even volunteered to wash me if I wanted.

I cannot have that happen again. I swear. Auntie has done enough. I know she means well, but her concerns make me feel weaker, more dependant, infantilised, disabled and even more victimised. Her excessive care keeps me stuck in a cycle of grief.

I am afraid to say this because she will take it the wrong way. She might see it as lack of appreciation for her efforts or might see me as an ungrateful spoilt brat who doesn't realise how lucky I am to have a comforter like her.

I fear that I might lose her if I tell her that grieving doesn't mean I'm disabled. As much as I need space form her, I need her. I will put up with her ICU-type care until I find a way to show her that I need some personal space if I am to heal properly.

I want auntie to stay as long as she wants not only for the healing process, but also because she might be the only thing standing in the way of getting a stepmother. I don't want this house to turn into Cinderella, with me being a slave to some mean woman and her bastard daughters. For as long as auntie is in the house, dad wouldn't dare.

Dad has a certain respect for auntie, the kind reserved for reverends and bishops. That means he will never get with auntie. A kind of upper grade friend-zoning. That means sooner or later, my life will turn into Cinderella. There is no shortage of women in *Venda* sniffing around, waiting for the second a wife loses her breath to occupy her side of the bed.

This is a place where single motherhood is rampant, men are no longer committal and marriage is an asset worth dying for. Women will go to the ends of the world just for the coveted title of *Mrs.*

I don't understand a woman like auntie who doesn't cease the opportunity while it's right next door. But wait until dad brings home a lady and she'll be jealous.

I remain in the corner of the dark dining room. I hear auntie flush. The toilet is that loud. She must have done the bigger job. Otherwise, we have all agreed in the house not to flush after peeing during the night. This is to avoid disturbing anyone's beauty sleep.

The flower vase on top of the drawer in the corner above me falls. It doesn't break but it blows my cover.

"Is anybody there? Hello," aunt calls out.

I hear her footsteps moving in the passage towards me. The rhythm she makes with her steps is not too different from mom's. Both could make good background to a chilled rap beat.

"Anybody in there?" she asks as she continues. I know she is carrying a broom. She keeps one in the passage, the bedroom, the back of the kitchen door and the entrance to the living room in the case of an intruder. So many brooms in the house. I have been meaning to ask her why, but I don't want to trigger some type of trauma I suspect makes her paranoid.

"Come out," she says in a brave, loud, yet shaky voice. I know she is scared but she will still defend herself.

"I am not afraid of you," she continues. "I will fight. Come out!"

"It's me, auntie," I shout before it gets ugly. "It's me in the dining room. Sorry to wake you up."

Auntie gasps in relief. "Mudangi? What are you doing here? Do you know what time it is? Huh? In the dark so alone?"

I get up from the corner where I was hiding. A *Mbue* novel on the dining table saves me. I quickly grab it.

"I...I...was, um," I struggle to make a quick story. I am not a good liar. I can go years without lying, you know? I'm that kind of a person.

"I was looking for, um, a novel," I continued. Auntie is already in the living room.

"I slept too early, and...I wanted to lull myself back to sleep by finishing this."

Auntie turns the light on in the dining room. She is standing under the arch that joins the dining room to the living room.

"Huh?" She does not hide her shock. "What? In the dark?"

The dim romantic lights start feeling like an interrogation light. I got caught. The walls might just as well close in on me.

"You scared me," said auntie. "Why are you in the dark?"

"Just looking for a book." I brisk past her, knocking her shoulder a little. "I found it. Don't worry. Let's go back to sleep." I raise the book as I rush back to the bedroom.

I am already halfway through the passage. She is staring at me. I know. I can feel her eyes on my back. I didn't even join eyes with her in fear she would see through me.

I am just about to enter the bedroom when she stops me on my tracks.

"Did you hear the footsteps again?"

I freeze. I got caught. I am at the door.

"Is mom back again?" Auntie is now standing next to me at the door. Nowhere to hide. Auntie sees through me. I hate it.

"Is she back?"

"Yes." I meant to say a big "NO," but my subconscious won the race.

"I will be okay!" I shouted and ran to my room. I shut the door behind me. On auntie's face.

"You know where to find me when you need me," said auntie. I can hear her crouched, projecting her voice through the keyhole. "It's gonna be okay. We'll get through this together, okay? I am here. It's all gonna be alright."

I hear her go to her room. She doesn't close her door. Her door is the squeakiest in the house. I would have heard if she closed it.

I lay on my bed in tears. Humbled.

"We'll get through this together, okay?"

Auntie's reassurance comforts me. With her, I know I will heal. I am not alone.

Ntendeni Luvhengo

Ntendeni Luvhengo was born and raised in the rural outskirts of Thohoyandou, Limpopo, South Africa. She lives in Johannesburg. A Rhodes University Bachelor of Journalism graduate, she is also a graduate of the Advanced Novel Writing Course from SA Writers College.

Two Children with a Book

This was the last time Lydie would see the portrait. As she walked into the saleroom of the auction house several faces turned towards her. Some eyes lingered – curious, questioning, amused – but most were retrained on the paintings which decorated the walls. She was certain there were no other governesses in the room, only collectors, artists, connoisseurs: the fashionable visitors to 8 King Street, St James' Square, and their friends.

Fifty of Emma's paintings adorned the walls of the auction house that week, listed as Lots 82 to 131 in the catalogue Lydie had picked up at the entrance. The cover read, "The Remaining Works of That Talented Artist, The Late Madame Soyer, Being a Portion of the Estate of the late Alexis Soyer... On Saturday, March 5, 1859."

Lydie and Grace's portrait, Lot 96, was to be sold.

It had served its purpose and would be in the hands of a new owner by the end of the auction. Lydie spotted it easily, hung between a picture of two boys selling lemons and a young girl nursing a terrier puppy. She hesitated. A couple stood before her. She could hear them proclaiming their sympathy, with heightened pity, for the unfortunate children in the paintings, adding their stage whispers to the hum of voices demonstrating each owner's supposed expertise. Lydie pivoted to a nearby painting of tulips and attempted to engross herself in their pale pink, yellow, white and lilac three-petalled bulbs resplendent against an almost black background, until the couple had gone.

She approached the double portrait. There she was with Grace, nearly thirty years younger, and encased in a slightly bruised golden frame. The younger version of herself on the canvas had her arm protectively wrapped around her little sister's shoulders. She was gazing up towards the heavens, as though inspired by the bible in her lap - Emma had said she'd look more pious that way. There were palm trees in the background, and behind them the setting was dramatic, vast: Bermuda.

"No one can deny you're two dignified young ladies." Emma had proclaimed.

The girls looked smart in the costumes Emma had chosen for them to wear. A simple blue and white striped smock dress with a paisley sash tied around the waist for Lydie, and a cotton two-piece yellow jacket and petticoat for Grace.

Emma had long since been buried in a cemetery in Kensal Green. Lydie's body had aged, and she wondered what Grace, now in Massachusetts, looked like today. But the painting remained unchanged, fixed in 1831.

Emma - first Miss Jones and then Madame Soyer after her marriage to Alexis - painted over 400 works in her short career, mostly portraits of one or two sitters with a variety of props such as instruments, fruits, flowers, baskets, brooms, sculptures and jewellery. Her other paintings were scenes of daily life: a lone pensioner seated at his table; a crossing sweeper clearing the path for a lady's skirts; women at harvest; and Lydie and Grace, two children, fourteen and eleven, with a book. They remained the only black sitters Emma ever painted.

They had met through Mrs Walker, Lydie and Grace's guardian, on the day of the first sitting. Mrs Walker was kind to the two girls. She was largely concerned with their moral welfare and education and so carried out a daily inspection of their needlework, scales and finger work on the piano, watercolours, and reading, writing and arithmetic. As the older sister Lydie was often the most carefully scrutinised. She had learnt the correct words to say to Mrs Walker, though she didn't feel it. On the days when their progress was of little importance to the middle-aged woman, she held the girls close to her on the emerald couch in the drawing room and read to them, filling their little nostrils with her scent of bergamot and lemon oil.

Mrs Walker belonged to three societies. One for the promotion of spiritual guidance amongst the poorer ladies of the parish. Another for the funding of a hostel for working girls in London. And the final for the relief of enslaved Africans, particularly enslaved women. She had left a luncheon for the latter roused by a new mission involving Lydie, Grace, Emma, and Emma's mother Madame Simonau, a fellow member of the society.

Lydie had fond memories of Madame Simonau and her occasional visits for tea. There was a softness to her when she asked about the children's lessons, or when she spoke of Bermuda. Lydie had gathered fragmented information about the tiny distant island, and her mother's life there, from Mrs Walker, Madame Simonau and other ladies from the Society for the Relief of the Enslaved.

A neat stack of the albums they produced on Bermuda and other Caribbean islands had stood tall on the mahogany desk below the portrait of the late Mr Walker in the drawing room. The stack grew by one album every few months. Lydie had read them all. The first she had found at seven. They contained reproductions of auction ledgers listing people who looked like her in the Caribbean. There were prints of men in chains on their knees begging, or squished into ships like fish in a barrel which caused Lydie nightmares for weeks. The content of the albums grew to include poems and songs in support of the abolitionists, and the society's annual reports. On Mrs Walker's suggestion, one album was to include a portrait of Lydie and Grace.

Madame Simonau and Mrs Walker introduced the two girls to Emma, then eighteen, at her home studio in Fitzroy Square. What Lydie always remembered about Emma was her poise and the attentiveness she had learnt from her mother. Windows covered one wall of the studio, making it cheerful and light.

Multiple paintings at various stages of completion were dotted around the room. Emma had shown the girls the linen canvas on which they were to be painted.

It was stretched taut over the wooden beams visible from behind, a bit like the smaller frame Lydie used when embroidering. A biscuit-coloured pigment had been applied evenly on the canvas. A *ground,* Emma had called it, to help prevent the painting from developing cracks or flaking off the surface. Thirty years later, Lydie couldn't see any paint losses. The image hadn't deteriorated.

"Would you like to stand over there?" Emma asked. She had gestured to a spot near a window in front of blue drapes, a stand-in for what eventually became the Bermudian landscape and palm trees she copied from an art book. A thick bible with a worn leather cover and cracked spine lay waiting by the windowsill. "Try kneeling, bow your heads, clasp your arms together as though you're praying," Emma had offered. Lydie and Grace complied and sank to their knees, Lydie already concerned about the pain of maintaining the position until Emma had what she needed. The girls had looked up at Emma, now towered above them, waiting for the next instruction. All three had felt uneasy.

"The position isn't right," Emma murmured and hesitated, unsure of what justification to give. "It looks too similar to the other images Mrs Walker and *maman* use," she finally invented. Lydie understood. "Perhaps we can sit on stools?" she had responded. Once they had found their positions, Lydie appreciated not having to meet Emma's eyes.

She let her mind wander - over the embroidery she had started the day before, her mother who she could not remember, the scrapbook of her favourite authors that she was making, and back to her mother again. When Grace became restless Emma encouraged her to walk around the studio imagining the lives of the sitters in the incomplete pictures. Lydie continued to pose for the portrait. Madame Simonau interrupted mid-morning with small pieces of cake and jam puffs. She paused to coo over Emma's sketch, then left the girls to continue.

"What was your *maman* like?" Emma asked.

"We can't remember her." Lydie answered, and offered nothing else. Emma understood. She continued painting, eyes flicking between the girls and the canvas. A clock in the distance chimed. It was time to leave. Lydie had not felt the morning pass.

They had sat for Emma every other day for three weeks. Lydie grew to enjoy the silence of Emma's studio and the time away from her lessons and minding Grace. They occasionally spoke. Emma explained it was usual for her to work on two or three paintings at a time. She had been exhibiting at the Royal Academy since she was ten. Mid-morning, Madame Simonau came in with refreshments as usual, then departed.

Lydie wondered how Emma saw her.

"Mrs Walker often says I look like mother," Lydie began one day. Grace was exploring the props Emma had recently added to the studio. "I catch her watching me sometimes."

Emma didn't interrupt Lydie. She wiped her palette knife clean and scooped up some blue paint. She listened to her new companion speak. Lydie felt the weight of the bible on her lap. It had fallen open to a chapter on one of the prophets at their first sitting. Emma diligently opened it to the exact same page at all sittings after.

"I came to London with mother and Mr Walker when I was a baby. Grace was about to be born." Emma swiped a layer of the blue paint onto the picture and Lydie continued. "Mrs Walker said it was safer here for mother." The palette knife scraped against the canvas.

Mrs Walker had described Lydie's mother as an herbal healer. She treated both Bermudians and the English gentlemen on the island.

"I listened in on Mr Walker once. He said the English gentlemen in Bermuda feared the men in their fields. And the cooks in their kitchens."

Emma picked up a thin brush to smooth the blue over.

Lydie had found out years after Mr Walker's conversation that her mother, a free woman, had been providing enslaved Bermudians with poisons for use against plantation owners.

Emma continued to work. They returned to a silence softened by the rhythm of the paintbrush against the canvas. "What happened to her?" Emma eventually asked.

"She died as Grace was born."

The same fate awaited Emma at 29, but her child would die with her.

A woman cleared her throat behind Lydie in the saleroom. She softened her face with a gentle smile and stepped forward, signalling to Lydie that it was her turn to view the painting. Lydie returned the smile and turned back to the portrait, wanting to spend a few more minutes with it. The woman moved on.

Chiedza Mhondoro

Chiedza Mhondoro is an art historian and curator. She specialises in the art of the eighteenth century and its wider, cultural, economic, political, and international contexts. Her creative writing blurs the line between fiction and history.

unleashed

It isn't until they approach the Eurotunnel that Alice realizes the doctors must have forgotten to cut the umbilical cord. Ever since leaving London, she has been feeling little tugs in the vicinity of her navel. At first she believed it to be the first stages of a bad case of flatulence. The pregnancy made her terribly insecure about her body, and she never learned to tell the baby's movements from those of her bowels. But the baby has been out for nine weeks, so telling should be easy, shouldn't it? It could be her hiatal hernia, of course – curtesy of a petite body and a giant baby. Part of Alice's stomach is now in her chest. Who knows what her other organs have been up to?

The tugging around her navel is new, though, and when Alice lifts her T-shirt, she sees the skin she grew to accommodate her daughter disappear down her bellybutton. She closes her eyes and opens them again. Surely, her navel's hunger is some optical illusion. Rays of light doing cartwheels on her skin? Raindrops on the window, refracted? Except, when Alice puts her finger in, it feels the same things it feels when she inserts it into her daughter's mouth.

Infinity.

Need.

With some force, Alice extracts the finger from her body's newest void. She stares at it. Blood. She encircles her bellybutton and counts the seconds it takes for the smear to disappear. Eleven. Is that fast? She's being removed from her daughter at a speed of approximately, what, 130 miles an hour? Should she start a log?

Reluctant to put her finger in a second time, she picks up the pencil she's been writing with and puts it in. Ten seconds – zero chances of extraction. Alice looks around to see if anybody has noticed. But she's on the first Eurostar of the day: nobody's noticing anything except their phones and inner eyelids.

Instead of wondering how many pencils she's got left, Alice supposes she should be freaking out. But freaking out requires energy and Alice has no energy. Alice hasn't slept for more than 30 minutes straight ever since the baby pushed part of her stomach up her chest.

Besides, it isn't *that* strange, is it? It makes sense she's only now noticing the umbilical cord is still – in place? Active? After all, these past nine weeks, she hasn't been away from her daughter for more than half a mile. 956 steps. The exact distance between Alice's flat and the creche. The purpose of the creche is to allow Alice to finish her dissertation. But all she's done so far is dozed off, only to wake up like a bad drunk, thinking she's smothered Edith or misplaced her. At times, it isn't until Alice puts her head in the oven, toilet and bin before she realizes her daughter is at the creche.

'Think,' Alice thinks.

There's not much extra skin left for her navel to take. What will it want next? Already, Alice's face is feeling more taut.

She decides to go and sit in the opposite seat – the tugging might just change direction. For an instant, she fears her navel will jut out like a giant erection. The thought almost makes her laugh. But no.

No erection.

Well, she thinks. If she is to disappear, outside in is probably better than insides out. Cleaner. People will wake up at some point.

***

Two days ago, Alice received a phone call from a Parisian hospital. As the consultant pronounced her name the French way, she failed to recognize it. Why was someone calling her to talk about *a lease,* or *a leash*? It took multiple back-and-forths for Alice's mind to swivel to her native French and even more to understand what the doctor was saying. Apparently, her mother had lost her language and Alice needed to come. Alice told the doctor it might take a couple of days to arrange the trip as she had a daughter of her own now. Alice hadn't had any plans to take Edith to France and she certainly didn't have any now. It would give her mother a proper scare, though: the woman didn't even know Edith was out. The doctor assured Alice the stroke hadn't caused anything life-threatening and that there was no need for her to hurry. But Alice's mother had taught her to not put off until tomorrow what she could do today, and the doctor had said the muteness was only temporary.

Until that call, Alice hadn't thought about her mother's body for years. Her mother became a voice the moment Alice moved to London to study. Not having to see her mother's monologues was a blessing, and whenever she had the chance, she took her mother's calls in the laundromat next door. The whirring and rumbling of the machines cut up her mother's diatribes into words that could be easily rearranged into harmless sentences.

Covid messed things up, though. Phone calls became a thing of the past. In came Zoom. And from a voice on the phone, Alice's mother once again became a presence that was hard to avoid. It was as if they'd gone back to the era of corded desk phones. Her mother did not take well to Alice moving around or doing other things when they were on Zoom.

She wanted her daughter to sit. She wanted her daughter to sit closer to the camera. She wanted to tell her daughter she looked tired. That she had a zit. No. Two zits. That it was clearly that time of the month again. Her mother had always been able to tell when Alice was bleeding, hadn't she? And why was Alice still not on the pill? And what on earth was going on with that shirt? Makes it look like she has tits sprouting from her hips. Does she really have nothing classier to wear? A bra, for starters? Does she actually want to find a husband? If she doesn't put in any effort, no man will, and men stop trying, Alice knows that, she should. And does she know how lucky she is she can go to college? Granted, a British college – but better a British college than no college, which is what her mother got. Nothing. Her mother got nothing. Well, she got Alice. So Alice should make her mother proud, and not get drunk, drunk doesn't look good on a girl, it looks dumb and easy and Alice is not easy -

Alice's mother is much but certainly no fool. Had Alice really expected her mother not to notice that was no tea in that mug? Alice's theatrical blowing gave her away: during one of the calls, she blew her wine so hard the splatter of saliva was audible in Paris.

The only good thing about Covid zooming was that everyone was zooming, which made the connection unstable enough for the screen to freeze and unfreeze every few seconds. It made her mother's mouth look like that of a ventriloquist dummy and it didn't require much additional imagination to see the resemblance between her mother's 17-inch head and that of a fortune teller machine in an amusement park. And Alice's mother did have a talent. In one of the Covid-intervals, Alice did meet a tall handsome stranger. And yes, Alice got drunk. She didn't ask the stranger if she'd been easy but getting pregnant sure had been.

***

They're almost in Folkestone and although the tugging hasn't stopped, it does seem to have eased. For the first time Alice wonders how her daughter's bellybutton is. Has the tugging become less intense because her daughter is now being dragged through the south of England in the wake of the Eurostar? It isn't difficult to picture her daughter floating. Only nine weeks ago, Edith was still blissfully weightless inside Alice's womb.

Alice takes out her phone and texts the creche for a picture. The picture comes fast. Too fast. Who's minding the babies? Somebody is: the picture is the same she received two days ago. Do they honestly think she doesn't know what her daughter is wearing?

Afraid to lose the connection she decides to Facetime rather than send another text.

'Show me her belly,' Alice says to the ear on the screen.

The ear throws the phone in the cot, leaving Alice to stare at a ceiling that looks like baby boys have been aiming their weenies at it for decades. Then, the snag of buttons, and finally. Edith. No bloodied pencil in sight. Just a perfectly innocent bellybutton: not an abyss, like Alice's, but a little bump in the shape of an ammonite.

Absolute.

The moment Alice realized what the yanking was, she had known her womb was innocent, that she wasn't luring Edith back – and now she knows neither is her daughter.

They're well underneath the channel and all connection is gone. Alice supposes she'll have to wait until they resurface to call – who, exactly? Not her silenced mother. The hospital, then, and ask them to lift her mother's nightdress, unbutton her pajamas. She should probably warn them against the bloodied pencil. Her mother isn't one to shy away from a good stab.

Sofie De Smyter

Sofie De Smyter is a student counsellor and English TA at KU Leuven (Belgium). Her words appear in *The Belfield Literary Review*, *Litro and Profiles*, amongst others. She was shortlisted for the Scratch A4 competition and longlisted for the 2023 Bath Short Story Award.

Will You DSM Me?

The Diagnostic and Statistical Manual of Mental Disorders (DSM)[1] *is the handbook used by healthcare professionals as the authoritative guide to the diagnosis of mental disorders. DSM contains descriptions, symptoms, and other criteria.*

*

The strangers on the city sidewalk flow assertively by me — an interweaving stream of faces that do not make eye contact. I am swept along by their collective current. For a moment, I imagine I am floating, carried forward upon their wake. I am the fallen leaf in the river, bobbing merrily along until I reach my final resting spot. This is oddly comforting. I am invisible.

Then their tide forces me to cross a large sewer grate. Or is it a subway vent? It spans most of the sidewalk, easily ten feet wide, its metal rungs moving and rattling just enough under my feet to trigger the image of one of the grill pieces shifting. *It will fall off its supports and send you down into the dark unknown below. Blackness and stank water await.* My intellect knows this is an irrational thought, but my heart's imagination does not and begins to race. I quicken my step, eager to get off the grate. Once back on solid pavement, I take a deep breath — I feel dizzy. *Do not pass out and make a spectacle of yourself!* I am fine. I am not crazy.

> *General Anxiety Disorder – Symptoms & Criteria for Anxiety*
> (3) *At least four symptoms out of the following list of items must be present, of which at least one from items (I) to (IV).*
> *(I) Autonomic arousal symptoms:*
> *(a) Palpitations or pounding heart, or accelerated heart rate.*
> *(II) Symptoms concerning chest and abdomen*
> *(e) Difficulty breathing.*
> *(III) Symptoms concerning brain and mind:*
> *(k) Fear of losing control, going crazy, or passing out.*

I enter the office tower, pulling my phone out as the door swings shut behind me to check the time. Just enough for a quick bathroom break before my committee meeting. Upon entering the washroom, I can hear a woman throwing up in the second stall. *At nine am, here?* I hold my breath until I reach the farthest stall. Not drunk, sick. *Could be contagious. People your age die from the flu all the time.*

(III) Symptoms concerning brain and mind:
(l) Fear of dying.

I hear her stall door swing open, then the tap running. I wait inside my stall until she leaves. When I exit, I lay a paper towel on the counter before placing my bag on top. I wash my hands carefully. *Too many people do not wash their hands.* My face looks waxy and tired, so I freshen my makeup. Once done, I pack everything in my bag, zip it shut, and wipe the counter with the towel. I start walking toward the exit.

You left something behind. You should check the counter. Do not go back, do not turn around! Struggling with my inner voice is impossible — I have to check. I walk back past the dryers until I can see the counter.

Nothing there.

*

At the end of my meeting, the committee Chair praises me for the pitch. He stands too close to me while he is talking, however. I can feel my left hand starting to shake, so I grasp it with my other hand. Steady.

"That one was a real walk in the park. Thanks again, Sandra, for all your work on this. I can always count on your research to find their secret weakness." He smiles, electrified our charity will receive an influx of much-needed funding. I cannot respond, so I look away. *Breathe.*

"They were thrilled," he adds. "I predict a big donation." I can feel his concern. Without making eye contact, I nod. I start moving papers around, pretending to pack up my notes. My mouth is too dry. *Where is your water bottle?* It is empty. I drank it during the meeting.

(I) Autonomic arousal symptoms:
(c) Trembling or shaking.
(d) Dry mouth (not due to medication or dehydration).

I manage to look at him. He frowns. "Good job, Sandra. Really." He pauses. "The other potential donor we spoke about contacted me yesterday. Having lunch with him today. I would invite you to join us, but maybe you should take the rest of the day off? You look tired. I'll send you his profile on Monday and we can strategize."

Oh no. I've done something wrong. Why doesn't he want me to come to the lunch meeting? *No matter what he says, you know he's thinking something else.* I suddenly feel nauseous. *Could you do more to help? Have you let him down somehow?* Maybe I've already caught something from the vomiting washroom woman. No. He likes my work. I am a talented researcher. I can read between the lines. I see things other people do not. I am a busy, successful person who kindly gives her time. He doesn't want me off the committee. *What if he thinks you're too quiet? Too outspoken? Does he think you're trying to replace him as Chair?*

> *(1) Excessive anxiety and worry (apprehensive expectation), occurring more days than not, about a number of events or activities*
> *(2) The individual finds it difficult to control their worry.*
> *(3) At least four symptoms out of the following list of items must be present, of which at least one from items (I) to (IV).*
> *(II) Symptoms concerning chest and abdomen*
>
> > *(h) Nausea or abdominal distress*
> > *(e.g., churning in the stomach).*

"Sure. Thanks, Steve. Let's talk Monday."

*

When I get home that evening, I curl up in my favorite armchair with my advanced Sudoku book — the effort to hold all those numbers in my head is calming. Clears my mind of all else within minutes.

Did you close the garage door? Is it wide open, inviting theft? No, I pushed the automatic garage door button. It is closed. I take the bookmark out of my Sudoku and pick up my pen. Only amateurs use a pencil. *Wouldn't hurt to check. You will feel better.* I get up, then walk quickly downstairs — as if my paranoia will go unnoticed if I am fast enough. I live alone, but still — I notice.

(1) Excessive anxiety and worry (apprehensive expectation), occurring more days than not, about a number of events or activities
(2) The individual finds it difficult to control their worry.

The garage is dark, its door closed. I close the access door and turn the lock. Two steps out of the mudroom, I cannot resist returning to pull on the door handle. Only once I feel the reassuring rattle of the deadbolt between me and the outside do I head back upstairs.

*

I set two alarms each night — one on my cell and another on an old-fashioned battery clock I've had since college. Just in case one fails. I have an abhorrence for lateness. As I turn off the bedside lamp, I cannot remember if I locked the front door. No, of course, it's bolted — I came in through the garage. *Wait, when was the last time you checked? Maybe you should check it. It is not safe to sleep with the door unlocked. Remember when the neighbour's home was broken into last year?* My mind is blank. I cannot recall the last time I used the front door. It is locked. I always lock it. I should stay in bed — I'm bundled in already. For a moment, I successfully resist the urge to go downstairs. Then there is an unexpected bang outside, causing me to sit up. I suddenly feel out of breath.

(IV) Other Non-Specific Symptoms:
(s) Exaggerated response to minor surprises or to being startled.
(t) Difficulty in concentrating or mind going blank because of worrying or anxiety
(v) Difficulty getting to sleep because of worrying.
(V) Symptoms of tension:
(p) Restlessness and inability to relax.
(q) Feeling keyed up, or on edge, or of mental tension.

It is my neighbour's husband, returning home late again. He tries to slip in quietly, but, more often than not, fails to navigate the trash bins in the alleyway. Still, I cannot fall asleep. *You should check the door. Safety first!* I slip out of bed in the dark, then glide down the stairs, my heart pounding.

(I) Autonomic arousal symptoms
(1) Palpitations or pounding heart, or accelerated heart rate.

It is locked. I feel much better.

*

The next morning, I arrive at the clinic fifteen minutes before my appointment. The office has just opened; the secretary is on the phone and doesn't look up when I enter. I glance at the shiny plaque on the office door:

> Dr. S. Hawking, M.D.
> PsyD, LGPC, MBBS.
> Licensed Psychiatrist.

I always thought it pretentious when people list their degrees after their names — trying to prove their worth. I can't understand why it is not sufficient to state "Licensed Psychiatrist." That title was hard enough for new patients to face all on its own without credential letters added, asserting their authority. Standard signage for such practices, however, or so I've been told. Recognizing the secretary is too busy to take notice of me, I turn the knob and enter the office, closing the door gently behind me so as not to disturb her call. Immediately, I feel restless. I have never been good at waiting. What to do until she arrives?

Placing my purse behind the largest chair, I flop down into its curved leather. I tell myself to remember to sit up straighter when she comes; best to make a good first impression. In the meantime, I can enjoy the way the chair seems to wrap itself around me. Like a cocoon. The swivel of its base sets me on edge a bit, however. I prefer to be more grounded. I uncross my legs, then plant both feet firmly on the floor. *That is much better.* I glance up at the clock. Five minutes to nine. Was she going to be late? Surprising. I see the blank notepad and pen the secretary has placed on the coffee table. I pick it up. It is thick, the hefty kind that I like.

The office door opens. A tall, thin woman enters the room. Her hair is pulled back too tightly in a strange high ponytail that defies its grey cast. She sits down across from me. I sit up straight, placing the notebook gently on my lap after quickly jotting a note about her promptness.

"Cathy. Nice to meet you. Please, call me Sandra. Why don't you tell me why you're here? Start anywhere you like. I'm here to help."

* *regarding DSM quotes throughout the piece. All indented text is taken from*

DSM, Symptoms and Criteria for Anxiety, as sourced from:
American Psychiatric Association,
www.psychiatry.org/psychiatrists/practice/dsm/feedback-and-questions/frequently-asked-questions, and
the DSM section for diagnosis of General Anxiety Disorder.

Cheryl Skory Suma

Cheryl Skory Suma is a multi-Pushcart nominee whose work has placed in 47 competitions since 2019. She is Flash CNF Contributing Editor at *Barren Magazine*.

Will You DSM Me was first published by *The Phare Magazine*.